STEELE'S WAR:
THE PREACHER

GW00758764

Other books by this author available
from New English Library:

EDGE 1: THE LONER
EDGE 2: TEN THOUSAND DOLLARS AMERICAN
EDGE 3: APACHE DEATH
EDGE 4: KILLER'S BREED
EDGE 5: BLOOD ON SILVER
EDGE 6: THE BLUE, THE GREY AND THE RED
EDGE 7: CALIFORNIA KILLING
EDGE 8: SEVEN OUT OF HELL
EDGE 9: BLOODY SUMMER
EDGE 10: VENGEANCE IS BLACK
EDGE 11: SIOUX UPRISING
EDGE 12: THE BIGGEST BOUNTY
EDGE 13: A TOWN CALLED HATE
EDGE 14: THE BIG GOLD
EDGE 15: BLOOD RUN
EDGE 16: THE FINAL SHOT
EDGE 17: VENGEANCE VALLEY
EDGE 18: TEN TOMBSTONES TO TEXAS
EDGE 19: ASHES AND DUST
EDGE 20: SULLIVAN'S LAW
EDGE 21: RHAPSODY IN RED
EDGE 22: SLAUGHTER ROAD
EDGE 23: ECHOES OF WAR
EDGE 24: THE DAY DEMOCRACY DIED
EDGE 25: VIOLENCE TRAIL
EDGE 26: SAVAGE DAWN
EDGE 27: DEATH DRIVE
EDGE 28: EVE OF EVIL
EDGE 29: THE LIVING, THE DYING AND THE DEAD
EDGE 30: WAITING FOR A TRAIN
EDGE 31: THE GUILTY ONES
EDGE 32: THE FRIGHTENED GUN
EDGE 33: THE HATED
EDGE 34: A RIDE IN THE SUN

EDGE MEETS STEELE: TWO OF A KIND

ADAM STEELE 1: THE VIOLENT PEACE
ADAM STEELE 2: BOUNTY HUNTER
ADAM STEELE 3: HELL'S JUNCTION
ADAM STEELE 4: VALLEY OF BLOOD
ADAM STEELE 5: GUN RUN
ADAM STEELE 6: THE KILLING ART
ADAM STEELE 7: CROSS-FIRE
ADAM STEELE 8: COMANCHE CARNAGE
ADAM STEELE 9: BADGE IN THE DUST
ADAM STEELE 10: THE LOSERS
ADAM STEELE 11: LYNCH TOWN
ADAM STEELE 12: DEATH TRAIL
ADAM STEELE 13: BLOODY BORDER
ADAM STEELE 14: DELTA DUEL
ADAM STEELE 15: RIVER OF DEATH
ADAM STEELE 16: NIGHTMARE AT NOON
ADAM STEELE 17: SATAN'S DAUGHTERS
ADAM STEELE 18: THE HARD WAY
ADAM STEELE 19: THE TARNISHED STAR
ADAM STEELE 20: WANTED FOR MURDER
ADAM STEELE 21: WAGONS EAST
ADAM STEELE 22: THE BIG GAME
ADAM STEELE 23: FORT DESPAIR
ADAM STEELE 24: MANHUNT
ADAM STEELE 25: STEELE'S WAR: THE WOMAN

STEELE'S WAR:
THE PREACHER

George G. Gilman

NEW ENGLISH LIBRARY/TIMES MIRROR

for
the Attrills
who are quick on the draw –
if you're fast with the money

A New English Library Original Publication, 1981
Copyright © 1980 by George G. Gilman

First NEL Paperback Edition January 1981

NEL Books are published by
New English Library Limited,
Barnard's Inn, Holborn,
London EC1N 2JR.

Made and printed in Great Britain by
Hunt Barnard Printing Ltd.,
Aylesbury, Bucks.

0 450 04661 3

AUTHOR'S NOTE

Although the two-part short story and flashback sequence in this book are complete in themselves, the events which they relate continue those which had their beginnings in *The Woman* – No. 25 in the Steele series

THE PREACHER

Part One

THE Reverend Saul M. Jarvis rasped the back of a dirty hand across the thickly sprouting bristles on his jaw and tried to spit out the taste of too much liquor and too many cheroots. The dusty soil of the Peloncillo Mountains' western foothills eagerly sucked in the saliva, while the man experienced the initial painful need for the first drink of the new day.

It was as yet only seven o'clock in the morning, but the sun was already high above the ridges which marked the Arizona–New Mexico territorial line in back of where Jarvis stood. High, hot and glaringly bright: threatening another long and uncomfortable day for the lone white man and the hundred or so Mescalero Apaches who shared the misfortune of living on the San Simon Rancheria.

Jarvis stood just beyond the open doorway of a one-room shack on the fringe of an expanse of crudely constructed wickiups, the occupants of which had stirred from their beds long before the white man staggered out into the sunlight. But it was not the noise of the Indians rising to face the new day that had brought Jarvis to softly cursing awareness; but rather the smell of woodsmoke and cooking that entered his nostrils and threatened to erupt the liquor-soured contents of his stomach.

But he got out of the fetid darkness of the windowless shack and managed to suck in fresh air before anything more substantial than bile rose into his throat. And now he drew back his lips to show a brief smile of satisfaction. For it was always a minor triumph for the Reverend Saul M. Jarvis when he was able to greet the new day standing erect and breathing regularly – instead of crouched on all fours fighting to draw in lungsful of air between body-wracking retches.

The preacher was an unappealing looking man, even when he smiled. He had the kind of face that lacked the ability of exuding any sort of charm: so that even the broadest of grins suggested his happiness was never spontaneous – was a carefully created mood with a preconceived and totally selfish aim.

It was the face of a fifty-year old man who had struggled a great deal to live so long. A thin face with small, dark, deep-sunken eyes and hollow cheeks. With a prominent bone structure and a short, thin lipped mouth in which lurked blackened teeth and a yellow tongue. The skin which contoured the sparse flesh of his features was also more yellow than brown, as a result of exposure to the elements and over indulgence in man-made vices.

He was a tall man whose painfully thin frame made him look taller than five feet eleven: an impression which was strengthened by the dark hue of the tight fitting cassock, which encased him from the grubby white dog-collar encircling his scrawny neck to his dirt-grimed wrists and booted feet.

'It is a good morning for you, holy man? Today you can eat the food I bring?'

Jarvis turned his head to look at the squaw who had come around the corner of the shack, carrying a bowl of steaming beans in both hands. She was young and unattractive, as undernourished and unkempt as the white man.

8

'When the day starts this well, it can only get worse,' Jarvis answered, his voice thin and reedy. 'Might as well set it on the right track by forcing down some of that slop.'

The squaw thrust the bowl at him, then turned and shuffled away. Jarvis eyed the profile of her breasts and the more pronounced curves of her hips with a leer twisting his lips. Then he spat into the dust again and began to spoon up the beans, chewing on them without relish as he gazed unseeingly out across the broad expanse of the San Simon Valley, which was beginning to shimmer with the slick mirages of the rising heat haze.

He had only half eaten the breakfast when a movement that was not a trick of the sunlight caught his attention. He cleared his mind of lascivious images of slim-bodied young white girls, to concentrate on the reality of whoever or whatever was coming across the valley floor toward him.

It was perhaps a full five minutes before his shortsighted eyes were able to receive a clear impression of a man on foot, leading a horse on which a woman was riding sidesaddle. Once he was certain that his eyes were not deceiving him, Jarvis spun around and rushed into the shack, becoming soaked with sweat as he frantically tidied his spartanly furnished living quarters – taking great care to hide the many empty and two full bottles of whisky under his narrow bed. Then he washed up and shaved – cursed just once when the blunted razor nicked his throat – and hand-brushed the loose dust from his cassock. The short, cropped, iron grey hair that sprouted from his head needed no attention.

Thus did the Reverend Saul M. Jarvis look at his undistinguished best as he stood on the threshold of his humble abode, eating cold beans while he watched the man, woman and horse advance up the long and shallow slope toward the San Simon Rancheria.

'Good morning and welcome to you, strangers!' he called brightly as the newcomers closed within two hundred feet of

9

him. 'We do not have much of anything here, but we shall be pleased to share it with you!'

Too low for Jarvis to hear her, Lucy Girard said: 'If you weren't just talking the other day, it seems we've come to the right place.'

Adam Steele glanced back and up at her with an easy grin and answered, 'Food smells as good as you looked when we danced before the music played. You reckon we can have breakfast before the wedding?'

Jarvis heard the woman's laughter and saw the remnants of the smile on the man's face as they came closer. He showed a broad smile of his own in return, which from a distance Steele and Lucy saw as merely an expression of warm welcome, as they looked away from the preacher to survey the rancheria.

It was not much of a place, but since they had been out on the barren land of south-eastern Arizona for a long time, their first impression was coloured by their experiences of the immediate past.

A scattering of wickiups erected to no pattern, with an open area at the centre where a communal cooking fire burned. On one side the mean adobe shack in front of which the preacher stood, and on another a larger single storey Mexican style building with a crudely painted sign over the door – *Indian Agency*. Beside this a rope corral in which a dozen or so scrawny, unshod ponies cropped at short, sun-browned clumps of dry grass. The Mescalero braves who sat singly, in pairs or groups outside the entrances of some wickiups, vastly outnumbered the ponies. And they, their squaws and the children looked as uncared for and dis-illusioned as the horses. The Apaches who did glance at the newcomers showed total disinterest as they returned to finishing their food. And there was no talk about them or anything else. There was little sound of any kind – as if the dark pall of smoke from the cooking fire which hung over

10

the encampment cast a shadow affecting the lives of everyone below.

'The lady and I will be grateful for some beans, feller,' Steele told Jarvis, as he came close enough to smell old sweat on the preacher's body and stale liquor on his breath.

'Be a pleasure,' Jarvis answered, his small, dark eyes seeking a glimpse of bare ankle as Steele helped the woman down from the gelding. Then he yelled something in the gutteral Apache tongue and spread a pious expression across his thin face before the strangers looked at him again.

'Ours to eat the food,' Lucy added.

'Both of you a long way from home,' Jarvis said. 'From the south-eastern states, by the way you speak.'

The squaw who had brought the preacher his breakfast now came around the corner of the shack again, carrying two bowls.

Steele said, 'Grateful to you,' and touched his hat brim as he took the bowl.

Lucy was nervous and the squaw was envious as the second bowl was passed from one woman to the other.

'Why don't you step inside?' the preacher invited. 'Can't offer you anything but shade and a place to sit down.'

Steele nodded and ushered Lucy across the threshold in front of him, noticing that their host was momentarily gripped by something akin to lust as the woman brushed by him. Then the eyes of the two met and Jarvis was suddenly afraid of the hard look that crossed Steele's face.

'Not offering you anything except our company, feller,' Steele said as he stepped into the fetid shade of the shack.

Jarvis swallowed hard and blurted, 'You're from Virginia, sir. Lady's from further south, I'd say. I've got an ear for accents.'

'Mississippi,' Lucy supplied as she looked around for a place to sit down.

'Here,' Jarvis said quickly, hurrying to push a low table

11

close to the side of the bed, still trying to regain his composure after being seen to show blatantly irreligious interest in the woman. 'Room for the both of you.'

As the two sat down, bottles clinked beneath them. And Jarvis was again disconcerted.

Steele grinned and offered, 'A man who lives way out here the way you do has to have some pleasure.'

'Much more a curse than a pleasure, I can assure you,' the preacher said grimly. Then he shook his head. 'But my problems are of no concern to you good people. Eat. Please eat.'

They did so, while Jarvis turned his back on them and knelt before a small, crudely fashioned altar in a corner of the room, head bowed and hands clasped in front of his chest. But his mind dwelt on thoughts far removed from worship, as he considered how he might profit by the arrival of the strangers.

The man had, at first glance, seemed oddly out of place in the great emptiness of the south-western territories – but this was an impression created solely by his choice of clothing. He wore an expensively cut, city-style suit of a light grey colour and beneath this a red vest and a lace-trimmed white shirt. On his head was a low-crowned and wide-brimmed black Stetson. His footwear was a pair of once smart, spurless riding boots, now scuffed as badly as his clothing was sweat-stained and dust-smudged. The grey kerchief around his neck and the black buckskin gloves that hugged his hands so tightly were much older than the rest of his outfit. He did not wear a gunbelt.

Inside the clothing was a man small of stature – he stood little more than five and a half feet tall – but there was more than a mere hint of ample strength in the way he moved and held himself. In repose his face suggested that he was in his late thirties, and yet his brief smiles and the momentary beat when he had shown dark menace, had made him look respectively much younger and years older.

It was a handsome face which, during his early adult life, had probably lacked character. A long face with regular features dominated by the inky black eyes. Clean-shaven, but with long sideburns which here and there showed a strand of the red which his cropped hair had been before it turned prematurely grey. With skin darkened by sun and wind, cut deep with lines which may have been fashioned as much by mental suffering as by the harsh treatment of the elements and the aging process.

The woman was about thirty. A redhead who was no taller than five feet three, with a build which, although slim, was most definitely that of a mature woman in the thrust of her breasts and the flare of her hips. And the high-necked, long-sleeved white dress she wore fitted tightly enough to emphasise this.

After a rigorous ride across the rugged floor of the San Simon Valley, she did not, of course, look her best. But with her long hair brushed and a little make-up on her green-eyed, clear-complexioned face, she would come close to being beautiful.

She spoke – and even spooned the beans from her bowl – in a manner that suggested she was a woman of breeding. A lady. Which was something Jarvis had not come across in many years.

Abruptly, he shook his head – trying with a physical gesture to rid his mind of thoughts about the woman. For lusting after her slender, white body would achieve nothing. Except frustration. And he returned his attention to plans whereby he might be able to satisfy a need of a different kind.

'The beans were very good, sir,' Lucy said, as she finished eating and the preacher rose unsteadily to his feet.

'And we're grateful for the quiet service,' Steele added wryly, as he rattled his spoon into the empty bowl.

'A man of the cloth as weak as I must constantly pray to the Lord for the strength and will to continue such a ministry as I have been chosen to conduct,' Jarvis answered, his attitude falling so short of piety that it came close to being self-pitying.

'The Indians,' Lucy said. 'They are no longer . . . they are Christians?'

Jarvis sighed. 'Some of them. Very few. But I am always striving for greater success in the work of the Lord. It becomes increasingly difficult though. You saw what this place is like. Wretched. My flock received many promises from the government in return for laying down their arms and settling peacefully on this rancheria. They were told they would be given much that the white man treasures, in return for adapting their ways to the ways of the whites.

'But all they have received is virtual imprisonment, with the cavalry detachment at Fort Blanding their guards, unproductive land to till, an almost barren hunting ground and an ill-stocked agency store run by a cheating Mexican who is hardly ever on duty.' He sighed again. 'It is no wonder that these once proud people have become as wretched as the place where they are forced to live. And a minor miracle that I have been able to convert a handful of these poor souls to the religion of the white man, who has shown not a jot of Christian kindness toward them.'

While Jarvis was intoning his tale of woe, Lucy began to fan a hand in front of her face, stirring the fetid air across her sweat-sheened skin. Steele remained impassive, and behind his inscrutable exterior pondered the end to which the tall, gaunt-faced preacher was aiming.

'Oh dear, there I go again. Burdening people with troubles of their own with the problems that beset my flock and I. You are weary after an arduous journey, Mrs . . ?'

'It's Miss, sir. Miss Girard. And this is Mr Adam Steele. He rescued me from a most terrible situation and kindly

14

agreed to see me safely to a town where I may catch a stage back east.'

She shot a sidelong glance at the Virginian as she finished the short explanation of why they were travelling together. It was just a look. Nothing more. It certainly asked no tacit question.

'Or maybe we'll get married, feller,' Steele said evenly. 'Reckon you're qualified to perform the ceremony?'

The preacher smiled broadly and there was an avaricious undertone in the expression. 'The Reverend Saul M. Jarvis, sir. Ordained as a minister in the Protestant Episcopal Church.'

'I'm a Protestant!' Lucy said quickly, making no attempt to conceal her excitement. And now there was nervous eagerness in her pale green eyes as they met the cool gaze of the Virginian.

'Calvinist,' Steele supplied. 'Lapsed awhile. Reckon no one needs conversion.'

'Wonderful, wonderful!' Jarvis exclaimed. 'It's been years since I conducted a service of matrimony.'

He seemed even more delighted than the woman at the prospect of a wedding, as he turned, threw open the lid of a tin trunk beside the simple altar and began to rummage through its contents. Then Lucy's face clouded over as she said softly:

'There's an awful lot else we have to find out about each other, Adam.'

It was the truth. They had met just a few days ago when, in an explosion of violence, Steele had taken her away from a bunch of sex-starved prospectors at an isolated way station out on the valley floor. She had got off the stage at the Gold Gulch stop in good faith – a mail order bride promised to one man. But she would have become the common property of every gold grubber in the Dos Cabezas Mountains, had Steele not intervened. Then, on the first

15

morning after their one horse ride away from Gold Gulch, the Virginian accepted her implied offer of gratitude that went beyond mere words. And on impulse – not normally one of his failings – he had suggested marriage.

Now, he replied, 'Reckon that'll give us plenty to talk about in the long winter evenings, Lucy.'

'Yes, here it is!' Jarvis exclaimed as he pulled a leather-bound volume from the trunk and blew dust off it. 'The Book of Common Prayer containing the form of the solemnization of matrimony.'

'So let's get to it,' Steele said as he rose to his feet.

'Pleasure!' Jarvis cut in quickly. 'I would like to ask a favour of you two good people.'

'I'll pay the usual fee, feller.'

The preacher waved away the response and concentrated his gaze on the smiling face of the woman. 'Miss Girard. Her wedding day is one of the most important in the life of a woman. Yes, and a man, too. And I ask that you allow me to do what I can to make this an unforgettable occasion for you. I ask this not entirely unselfishly, I must admit. I would like time to prepare that part of the Indian Agency which serves as a mission church here. Time for those few converts I have made to explain what is to happen to their brothers and sisters. Hopefully so that we will have a large congregation who will be impressed by what they witness. And who knows, perhaps some of these wretched souls will see the light and want to discover more about the word of the Lord?'

His excitement mounted as he explained his request. Then, when it had been made, his small, dark eyes switched anxiously back and forth between the seated woman and the standing man. Lucy looked up at Steele, ran fingertips across her sweat-shiny forehead and then touched her disarrayed hair.

'I would like to take the time to clean up a little, Adam,'

she said. 'A bride should look her best.'

The Virginian gave no sign that he had heard her, for he had turned his head to squint out into the harsh sunlight beyond the open doorway. And now Lucy and the preacher also heard the sound that had captured his attention – the galloping hoofbeats of many horses. Approaching the rancheria from the south-east.

'It will be a patrol from Fort Blanding,' Jarvis supplied and there was a newer, deeper anxiety in his tone now. Then tightly controlled anger when he added, 'During their short visits here, the army manage to completely cancel out whatever progress I have made with these poor wretches.'

Steele appeared not to have heard Jarvis either as he moved around the table and stepped across the threshold of the shack, halting beside the gelding, saddled Western-style with a forward-slung boot from which jutted the fire-scarred rosewood stock of a Colt Hartford revolving rifle. He looked across the bedroll toward the patrol of a dozen blue-uniformed cavalrymen, as they slowed their mounts to a walk at the edge of the Apache encampment.

The patrol was composed of ten troopers, a sergeant and a lieutenant, riding fresh horses and showing only a scattering of trail dust on their smartly pressed tunics. The men moved in well-drilled formation, responding in unison to the officer's hand signals. Each of their faces was set in an expression of arrogant superiority with an undertone of disgust, as they rode double column between the wickiups toward the open area at the centre of the encampment.

Steele moved away from his gelding to the rear of Jarvis's shack, where he had a clear view of the patrol as it halted close to the embers of the communal fire. Other eyes watched with a keener interest than those of the Virginian. The Mascalero braves from in front of their wickiups, and the squaws and the children who had been ordered into the lodges.

'There's going to be trouble,' the preacher said softly as he and Lucy came to flank Steele. 'This isn't just a routine visit.'

'Red Bull, get your ass out here!' the big built, short-necked sergeant yelled. 'At the friggin' double!'

Lucy had not needed to hear Jarvis's warning – she had seen from the bellicose attitude of the cavalrymen and the tense stances of the Apaches that all was not well. And now she fastened a grip on Steele's forearm and dug her fingers into the fabric of his jacket sleeve.

'We're just passing through,' the Virginian muttered softly, as an elderly Apache flanked by two braves in their middle years emerged from a wickiup slightly larger than the rest.

'That's Chief Red Bull and his twin sons,' Jarvis said in a whisper. 'The sub-chiefs are waiting for their father to die and then they'll lead all these Indians back on the warpath.'

'What do the pony-soldiers want of me?' Red Bull asked, and his voice was as frail as his physique.

The faces of his look-alike sons were stoic under the steady gazes of contempt from the mounted men. But then expressed curiosity as the short, potbellied lieutenant took an envelope from inside his tunic and threw it down at the feet of the Apache chief.

'That's a warrant for the arrest of one of your people named Joe Starlight, Red Bull. The commanding officer of Fort Blanding has ordered me to bring in the man Starlight. I order you to deliver him to my custody.'

It was obvious which brave the patrol had come to arrest, since for varying lengths of time every Apache had been looking toward one of their number. A taller than average Mescalero who stood before a wickiup close to the Indian Agency building. A handsome brave in his early twenties who was obviously taken totally by surprise at the sound of his name. Then was angry, as he snapped a response to something which his squaw groaned from inside the wickiup behind him.

'Why is this?' Red Bull demanded.

'So the stinkin' sonofabitch can be hung!' the sergeant snarled.

This drew a chorus of shouted questions from all sides.

'I told you I'd handle this, Sergeant!' the lieutenant bellowed, and the words signalled a silence. He grunted his satisfaction, then moderated his tone to address the chief. 'The charge is rape and murder, Red Bull.' Another burst of angry voices, which he curtailed this time merely by raking his hard eyes over the culprits. 'Of Mrs Helga Traynor, the wife of the quartermaster at Blanding.'

'How you know this brave did . . . ' one of the sub-chiefs started.

'The accused will be put on public trial at the fort!' the officer cut in impatiently. 'All the evidence will be produced then. And Starlight will have a right to legal counsel who may challenge such evidence. Now, you have there the sworn out warrant for his arrest. Are you going to comply with my request?'

'Or are we gonna have to take the murderin' savage by force?' the sergeant asked bitterly – obviously relishing the prospect.

All eyes were now on the frail old chief, and it was obvious that the majority of braves were eager to pick up the guantlet tossed down by the short-necked sergeant. The dilemma tormenting Red Bull temporarily drained his physical strength and he swayed – might have fallen, had not his sons lent him steadying hands. He welcomed their help for a few moments. Then shook free and yelled:

'White eyes holy man! You come read me what this paper says!'

Attention swung again, this time towards the group of people standing behind the preacher's shack.

'Who the hell are you two?' the sergeant snarled.

'Keep your foul mouth closed, Turner!' the lieutenant

19

roared, anger colouring his face purple. Then he sucked in a deep breath and touched the brim of his hat. 'Allow me to apologise for the untoward language, ma'am. We were not aware there was a lady present.'

'Seems to me there's a lady in almost every lodge on this rancheria, Lieutenant,' Steele answered.

'Another Injun lover,' a trooper said in a stage whisper that carried to every ear, as his officer bristled at the taunt.

'Mr Steele and I are merely passing through, sir,' Lucy called, and tightened her grip on the Virginian's arm. Then hissed softly: 'It's what you said we were doing, Adam.'

The lieutenant became hard-eyed as his pallor returned to normal and he turned in his saddle to glare again at Red Bull. 'Jarvis can read it to you after we've left. If he's not too drunk to see straight. Now, tell Starlight to come quietly. Or I will not accept responsibility for the condition in which he reaches the fort.'

He rested a gloved hand on the hilt of his sabre. His men took this as a signal to unfasten their hip holsters and fist hands around the buts of the revolvers they contained.

The Apaches carried no guns – only hunting knives and tomahawks hanging from their weapon belts.

Tension seemed to have a crackling presence in the hot morning air. And when Steele shot a glance at Jarvis the preacher was visibly shaking with fear. Stretched seconds slid silently into history.

The officer snapped, 'Sergeant Turner.'

'Sir?'

'Take two men and bring the accused here. Trooper Wilmot.'

'Sir?'

'Fetch a pony for the prisoner to ride.'

Four men broke away from the group and, without dismounting, went to carry out the orders.

Apache eyes, smouldering with anger on a short leash,

20

switched between the uniformed army men and their chief and sub-chiefs.

'Let them take him, Red Bull!' Jarvis shouted in his reedy voice. 'I'll make sure he gets his legal . . .'

It was the twin son to the right of his father who took advantage of the diversion caused by the preacher's words to yell a one word order in his native tongue. Signalling the launch of a plan which had obviously been prearranged to counter just such a situation as this.

Upwards of twenty guns were thrust out of the entrances ·of wickiups; to be accepted by hands spread ready to receive them. Rifles and carbines. Repeaters and single shot weapons.

Red Bull started to scream a pleading counter order to the command of his son, only to be lifted easily off his feet and tossed back into his lodge. Against a barrage of gunfire that drowned out the old man's words and the scream of pain he vented as he hit the ground inside the wickiup.

All the shots were fired by the Apaches, who used the element of surprise to lethal effect. Half the cavalrymen were cut down by the first hail of bullets, plunging off their horses with more than one wound spreading dark stains across their uniforms or gushing blood from holes in their heads. Then the panic of the survivors and their mounts alike hampered attempts at retaliation, as the braves with repeaters levered fresh rounds into the breach and picked new targets. In under five seconds the entire patrol had been wiped out without firing a single shot.

And only then did the Apaches take evasive action – leaping clear as horses with bloodstained saddles and coats bolted across the encampment, nostrils flared to the stink of newly spilled blood and acrid gunsmoke.

'Dear God in heaven, it's happened!' Jarvis cried, swinging his head to look at Steele and seeing that both the Virginian and the woman had left him.

Against the beat of galloping hooves, a trooper screamed his pain and terror. A brave without a gun drew and hurled his hunting knife. The white man died. Whoops of triumph filled the air and then subsided under an onslaught of words bellowed in the Apache tongue.

The two sub-chiefs were doing the shouting and were in turn silenced by their father as he came out of the lodge – unsteady on his feet, but with his face set in an expression of hard anger.

Jarvis turned his head still further and saw Steele come around the rear corner of the shack, the rifle from the saddle boot now canted to his left shoulder. The Virginian's time-hewn face revealed nothing of what he was thinking. Behind him, the wan features of Lucy Girard were contorted by deep terror.

'Don't provoke them and they won't harm us,' the preacher said, the trembling of his body extending to his voice.

'Oh,' the woman exclaimed with no more than an outrush of breath as she squeezed her eyes shut against the sight of the bloodstained bodies sprawled on the arid ground among the wickiups.

Red Bull launched into a lengthy address to the braves, who for the most part listened shamefaced to what he said. The elderly chief seemed to gain strength as he achieved the response he was seeking. Then, as he concluded, the braves with guns shuffled to the entrances of their wickiups and handed the weapons back to the squaws inside.

'White eyes!' the chief called in English. 'You with the holy man!'

'I hear you Red Bull!'

'What has happened here is no concern of yours! My warriors have set aside their arms! You will set aside your rifle! If you do not, you and your woman will die!'

Steele felt Lucy's clawed hand gripping hard to his arm

22

again. He raked his dark eyes over the faces of the scattered Mescaleros and saw the potential for new killing in every one of them.

'Do it, please!' the preacher pleaded huskily, the sweat of fear running down his gaunt face.

'Seems we have deadlock rather than wedlock,' the Virginian growled. 'But the answer has to be the same.'

'How say you, white eyes?' Red Bull demanded, as every brave turned fully to gaze menacingly at Steele, and some of them made to start toward him as he shifted the Colt Hartford away from his shoulder. But they halted when he reached out and leaned the rifle against the side wall of the shack.

And murmured, 'I will.'

STEELE'S WAR

Book Two

CHAPTER ONE

IT was mid-May 1862 and Lieutenant Adam Steele was feeling good for the first time since he, and every other Confederate soldier who had survived the bloody carnage of the battle of Shiloh, had been ordered to withdraw from the ravaged and body-strewn west bank of the Tennessee River.

Shiloh had been the young cavalry officer's first taste of a major engagement in the War Between the States. And only now, as he lay sleepless in his bedroll on the bank of another river, was he able to ponder the events of some five weeks ago and consider himself satisfied. Not with the way the battle had been fought and certainly not with the outcome – but with his own conduct.

'Sir, you awake?'

Steele opened his eyes as the words were spoken and a hand shook his shoulder, and saw a man stooping over him – just a dark silhouette against the moonlit sky above encircling treetops.

'Sergeant Perry, sir. Report from the picket on the north perimeter. There's a group of men heading this way.'

Steele threw aside his covering blanket and got to his feet, glanced around quickly and saw that every other man not on picket duty was also awake. Standing or seated among the blankets of their bedrolls, they were looking toward the lieutenant as expectantly as Perry.

'How many, Sergeant?'

'Maybe a dozen, sir. No more.'

The non-com, who was a head taller than the officer and at thirty was some five years older, merely expressed expectation on his round, clean-shaven face. He had been under Steele's command at Shiloh, and had witnessed nothing which showed the lieutenant to be any better or worse than other officers of similar rank and inexperience. And during the orderly withdrawal from the battle, when there was time for reflection on and talk of the engagement, James Perry had come to respect Steele's views concerning a soldier's duty in the army chain of command. Not least because he shared them.

But the other troopers, who had been resting beside the line of five stalled wagons in the clearing on the east bank of the Mississippi, revealed, behind their tense expressions, feelings which ranged from apprehension to distrust, scorn to malevolence. Regular soldiers, volunteers and conscripts alike: they waited to see how this rich dude in uniform would respond to a potentially dangerous situation.

'Have a man inform all the pickets to maintain their watch and remain in position unless ordered otherwise, Sergeant,' Steele said evenly. 'Rest to stand by their assigned wagons. Armed.'

'Marks, pass on the Lieutenant's order to the pickets!' Perry snapped. 'Rest of you heard the Lieutenant! Do like he says!'

While the men complied, Steele stooped to pick up his hat and Spencer. Then beckoned for the non-com to follow him as he strode along the line of wagons. A few disjointed phrases reached his ears, before he and Perry moved out of the clearing and into the wood: the men voicing their views about him as they followed his orders. But he found it easy to stem his rising anger, by reflecting again on the train of thought which had engaged his mind before Perry had interrupted him.

Service in the army was a job of work which many chose to do. In time of war, many more men were either forced to take up the trade or felt compelled to don the uniform and bear the arms. Whatever the circumstances, such a mixture of men were required to give of their best within the limits imposed upon them, not by ability but by rank.

At the relatively minor engagement of Rich Mountain, Adam Steele had been merely a civilian in lieutenant's uniform. The son of one of the wealthiest and most powerful men in the state of Virginia: experienced in running an extensive cotton and tobacco plantation where only his indulgent father had been in a position to countermand his orders.

At Rich Mountain he had experienced the same brand of bitterness which he had just seen in the faces of the troopers back at the clearing. Perhaps to a greater extent than they did, since as a junior officer he shouldered the burden of responsibility for carrying out the orders of his superiors. Superiors whom he had no reason to trust, respect or like; in the same way that the men under his immediate command were suspicious of his untried abilities.

But during treatment in a Richmond hospital and then while he held down an administrative post, he had come to terms with this inevitable problem. And thus fought the battle of Shiloh in a new frame of mind.

It was war: evil and bloody. A world removed from working on a peaceful plantation. And he was not the top hand: in this context he rated no higher than Elroy, the Negro who had headed up the slaves back on the Steele plantation. He had no way of influencing the decisions made by high command, and no longer took the time nor had the inclination to be concerned with what the men in his troop thought of him. Not if he was to carry out his resolve to do his lowly job as best he could.

'Well, will you look at that, sir?' the picket posted on the fringe of the trees a hundred yards north of the clearing said, with a broad grin as Steele and Perry reached him. 'Them folks are all female.'

The two newcomers peered from out of the moon-shadowed timber, along a turnpike that ran between the river bank and an area of high grass meadowland. Both the lieutenant and the sergeant had looked out at the same stretch of country earlier, while the men were preparing themselves and the horses for a night of rest in the clearing.

The turnpike was the same one they had been travelling for two days, moving north from Memphis with the ammunition-laden wagons bound for Fort Pillow. It swung in a half-circle around the stand of timber and, while night camp was being established, the two men had come forward to check the kind of terrain that would face the supply train when it set out at dawn.

Earlier, the semi-marsh landscape had been empty of any sign of life except waterfowl. Now, as they listened to the young trooper's voice with its tone of subdued excitement, Steele and Perry saw a group of women coming along the turnpike – four of them hauling a handcart.

'Quiet, Jones,' Steele rasped.

'But . . .'

A hard-eyed glare from Perry sufficed to make the trooper swallow his objection. Then all three men concentrated their attention on the group of women, who remained nothing more than dark silhouetted figures against the moon-whitened turnpike, until they were within twenty yards of where the Confederate cavalrymen watched and waited. Then the various colours of their gowns became visible, the blondes were distinguishable from the darker haired women and their figures and features took shape. There had been no talk among them: just the sound of their footfalls and the creak of the cart's turning wheels.

They advanced a further five yards, then came to a shuffling halt when a woman said distinctly:

'Hold it, girls. I figure they can see and hear us clear from here.' One of the three blondes stepped away from the group and raised her voice to shout: 'Hey, you fellers! Me and the ladies of Attrill have brought some comforts for the troops! We come closer, you won't start shootin' at us, will you?'

'Well, I'll be,' Trooper Jones rasped softly.

'You'll be friggin' quiet, soldier!' Perry countered, his voice quieter but stronger.

'Aw, come on, you can hear what I'm sayin' to you!' the spokeswoman shouted. 'We got good eats, a few bottles and ourselves! That's all we got and none of that can harm you fellers!'

Steele knew of the town of Attrill: had seen the name on the map that was now folded neatly and resting in a pocket of his tunic. It was the only community of any size on the turnpike between Memphis and Fort Pillow. Two miles north of their present position – just beyond the rise that marked the horizon. A rise he surveyed now, seeing no movement on the line where the land met the sky. To the left, the river flowed smoothly between its reeded banks. To the right, the tops of the long grass swayed in the gentlest of breezes.

He signalled Perry and Jones to remain in cover and stepped forward, showing himself in the moonlight beyond the shadows of the foliage. His abrupt appearance drew gasps of surprise from some of the women.

'Grateful to you ladies,' he called. 'But my men and I have adequate supplies.'

'Evenin' to you, son,' the blonde greeted. 'You mean you don't want what we brought you?'

'That's right, ma'am. We have a long way to go tomorrow and we need to rest up now.'

'But we come a couple of miles out of the goodness of our hearts. To show our appreciation of what you fine men are doin' to chase the damn Yankees out of the south.'

'That sure is the truth!'

'Yeah.'

'Yes.'

'Come on, mister, don't be so mean to us.'

'And your men.'

The chorus of agreement with the spokeswoman and complaints against Steele masked the sounds of footfalls in the timber. And neither the lieutenant nor Perry and Jones were aware of other men on the fringe of the stand until one of them exclaimed:

'Am I seein' things, Joe?'

And another answered, 'If you are, boy, you get the hell outta my dream!'

Steele felt the searing heat of temper rising from the pit of his stomach and this time was unable to check it. The emotion caused his voice to quiver when he yelled, 'Sergeant, send those men back to their posts! And put them on officer's report!'

'Damn it, Lieutenant! We could get our asses shot off by the bluebellies tomorrow! We gotta make the most of . . . '

Steele whirled around. 'Place that man under close arrest, Sergeant!' he snarled. Then flung over his shoulder, 'You women, get the hell back to where you came from! Jones, if any one of those civilians takes a step closer, consider her the enemy!'

'You mean for me to . . . ?'

Steele started back into the trees.

'Kill her, trooper!' he snapped, as shock trapped the words in Jones's throat.

'Hand me your carbine and side arm, Patterson!' Perry rasped.

'Up your butt, Sarge!' the trooper who had ignited Steele's rage snarled. 'I've had enough of takin' shit from snotnoses with fancy braid on their friggin' coats! You try to take . . . '

More troopers had come in the wake of Patterson and Joseph Harmer to see what was happening at the northern fringe of the timber for themselves. And Steele saw them – at least ten – standing in a two-deep arc behind Perry and Patterson, as he came to a halt beside Jones and Harmer. Fear of the situation showed on all their faces in the dappled moonlight filtering through the treetops. The two men who were the centre of attention expressed the same degree of anger that continued to grip Adam Steele.

'Johnnie!' Harmer croaked.

'It was my order, Trooper!' Steele snapped.

At this moment Perry leaned forward and reached out to take hold of Patterson's Spencer by the barrel.

Patterson broke off his tirade, was silent for a second, snarled, 'I told you!' Then he thumbed back the hammer and squeezed the trigger.

The sergeant took the bullet between his lip and nostrils, over a range of no more than eighteen inches. On an upward trajectory. So that the lead had the velocity and direction to burrow a gory tunnel through the flesh, tissue and bone of his head and burst clear at the crown. And enough power to jerk him rigidly erect to his full height before he died, became limp and crumpled to the damp grass and leaf mould.

Steele was shocked into immobility to the same degree as every other man who had witnessed the killing. And a fraction of a second slower to recover than Trooper Harmer.

'No, sir!' the eighteen-year-old volunteer enlisted man exclaimed sharply, jabbing the muzzle of his carbine into the small of Steele's back.

His words and the feel of the circle of metal against his spine caused the lieutenant to freeze again – in the act of bringing his Spencer to bear on Patterson.

'Dear God, what's happening?' a woman cried.

Patterson had been staring fixedly down at the inert corpse of the sergeant, and only now tore his eyes away from the victim of his impulsively lethal act. To swing his head from left to right, an incredulous expression on his face.

'We didn't want to cause no trouble!' the blonde woman who had done most of the talking called out.

Patterson looked on the verge of a trembling spasm as he stared around at the stricken faces of the other troopers. Then he saw Steele under the threat of Harmer's carbine, did a double take, and grinned.

'Sonofabitch!' he growled through his clenched teeth. 'Attaboy, Joe!'

'It's just to stop any more killin', Johnnie,' Harmer forced out through his constricted throat. 'We can't . . . '

Steele had been struggling to check a newer and more intense anger since the young trooper got the drop on him. A rage compounded of responses to every aspect of the situation that now faced him. The women for coming here, Sergeant Perry for not taking more care, Patterson for the killing, Harmer for his active support of the older trooper and the rest of the men for their tacit fence sitting. Most of all, though, he blamed himself: for as commander of the troop he should have exerted the kind of authority over the men which would have made the development of such a situation impossible.

'Any man who aids the murderer will be as guilty as he is,' the lieutenant said grimly, his voice cold and steady, raking his eyes over the faces of the troopers. Patterson stood beside the sprawled and inert corpse of the non-com. Steele stepped away from the pressure of Harmer's carbine and canted his own Spencer to his shoulder.

34

Patterson, who was a thirty-year-old ex-roustabout from the New Orleans waterfront, held his ground. He splayed his feet, raised his broad shoulders and widened his grin as he switched his grip on the Spencer – to hold it by the barrel in the manner of a club.

'One more won't make no difference, mister,' he rasped. 'To me or any of the boys who are sick of takin' orders from you, you jumped up little snotnose of a rich man's son.'

'You women, stay back!' Jones shouted, his voice shrill with tension. 'I got orders to . . .'

'The Lieutenant ain't givin' the orders no more, Harry!' Patterson cut in. And swung the carbine high and wide as Steele halted three feet in front of him. 'Them that are officers gotta be gentlemen, too. And a gent wouldn't treat ladies the way he is. Tell them to come on over.'

Cold fear swamped Steele's hot temper as he flicked his eyes across their sockets – seeking signs that at least some of the troopers behind the arrogantly defiant Patterson were prepared to back him. But he saw only apprehension in the pale faces, and was certain that their lack of positive response doomed him to die – for he had committed himself to a course of action that depended upon their support. With a sharp intake of breath, Patterson started to swing the Spencer stock toward his head – there was no chance of evading it by going forward to the attack or by throwing himself backwards.

He could only try to defend himself by whipping his own carbine away from his shoulder – into the path of the viciously aimed gun become club.

'No!' Joe Harmer screamed.

The single word resounded in a seemingly unending series of echoes between the inner walls of the Virginian's skull. The moonlit scene before his eyes tilted at a crazy angle. Then the monotonous sound of the young trooper's voice became shriller in tone, faded into the distance and was cut

35

short by the crash of one carbine stock against the barrel of another. A bolt of searing agony forced Steele to shut his eyes to the sight of the men he had failed.

He tried to open them again, but it was just not possible. Not possible, either, to understand what had caused the pain and the darkness: since his countermove with the carbine had parried the clubbing action of Patterson's Spencer.

The pain eased, but not the total blackness. A voice said, 'You'd have killed him.' Another responded, 'So friggin' what?' A woman gasped, 'Oh, this is terrible.' Adam Steele thought he said, 'It's worse than that, ma'am.'

Or maybe he merely thought it . . .

CHAPTER TWO

THE darkness without pain seemed to last for just a few seconds to be followed by an eternity of blindness in which the misery of agony was all that existed. Suffering so great that the mind was incapable of considering any idea that a thousand and one disjointed words might have triggered, as they came and went like lightning flashes through the intense dark.

War . . . death . . . hell . . . Diana . . . Elroy . . . murder . . . home . . . Bish . . . Richmond . . . Shiloh . . . father . . . wagons . . . Pillow . . . officer . . . sergeant . . .

'Attaboy, Joe! You're doin' fine, kid! All you gotta do is keep it up!'

Steele recognised the gleeful, slightly slurred voice of Trooper John Patterson. Then heard whistles and cheers, squeals and laughter. Pain continued to assault him and he felt the flesh of his face contort in reaction to it. But his mind was no longer totally filled by suffering – was again capable of logical thought and clear recollections.

He smelt damp grass and woodsmoke, hot food and strong liquor, burning tobacco and perfume. The sounds of people – men and women – enjoying themselves became clearer. He was aware of constraints that had more substance than the disabling effects of pain. Realised, as he received a vivid impression of what had happened to him on the fringe of the wood, that his hands were tied behind him, his ankles were lashed together and there was a gag over his mouth.

He cracked open his eyes.

It was still night, but a fire was burning brightly in the clearing beside one of the supply wagons. And he saw by its dancing light the reason for the explosion of gleeful sound that had roused him from unconsciousness.

The young Joseph Harmer, fully dressed but with the front of his pants open, was sprawled between the splayed legs of a naked woman: his buttocks rising and falling rhythmically, while his arms were clasped around her shoulders and his face was buried in the crook of her neck.

On either side of the coupling trooper and woman, the audience continued to shout encouragement and vent their laughing enjoyment of the obscene exhibition. Men and women with arms around each other. Men without women drinking liquor from the bottle, smoking cigars or chewing the meat they tore from turkey drumsticks.

Patterson and Jones. Phil Schneider and Don Groves. Greg Bluell and Arthur Harvey. Every other member of Steele's troop – except for Sergeant Perry, of course. All with names which the Virginian could have recalled if there had been reason to make the effort. But there was no such reason, for who they were was immaterial at this moment.

It was enough to know what they were – a troop of cavalrymen who had mutinied in time of war, murdered a comrade, made a captive of their officer and engaged in a drunken orgy.

The sounds of drunken and lustful hilarity rose in volume as the cadence of Harmer's thrusting movements increased toward climax. And Steele felt sick to his stomach: the nausea not aroused by the obscene event he was witnessing but rather by a sense of personal failure.

He closed his eyes to shut out the scene in the clearing: in

38

order to concentrate his entire being on the effort to fight back the sickness.

The noise continued to assault his ears and great beads of sweat oozed from his pores and trickled across the flesh of his face.

'That's it, Joe!'

'Go on, boy!'

'Screw the ass off her!'

'Get it over with and let your buddies take their turn!'

Steele was lying on his side, the small of his back against the stump of a long-felled tree and his legs folded up so that his thighs pressed to his belly. He had viewed the scene at an odd angle, the loll of his head causing the excited onlookers to appear strangely tall and powerful. And for the first time, when he re-opened his eyes after driving back the threat of nausea, he considered the possibility that he was still unconscious – felt like a disembodied pair of eyes gazing upon some fantastic image of a bad dream created within his own mind. But then he realised that a man experiencing a nightmare was unable to reason between such alternatives. And this was borne out when his eyes met those of the naked woman who lay submissively beneath the pumping body of the trooper.

She was sprawled out on her back parallel to Steele, some twenty feet away from him: her head to the side, so they could look at each other in a manner that did not distort what each saw of the other.

It was for this reason that the Virginian did not have to check his first impression of the expression on her face. The face of a woman who was old enough to be the mother of the teenage trooper who was taking her. A face which still retained traces of a one-time beauty that had been banished by a thickening of the flesh and the inroads of wrinkles. A face framed by cropped red hair, that showed an expression of deep shame – which took a firmer grip on the full features as the boy shuddered to his climax, emptied his lust into her and collapsed into heavy breathing limpness.

'All right, boy, let a man show you how it should be done!'

This from Don Groves, a farmer from Georgia who at forty-five was the oldest man in Steele's troop: shouted in a spray of spittle as he threw down a bottle, ran to the couple and stooped to drag the groaning Harmer off the woman.

'You ready for the best you've ever had, Gloria?' Groves roared, as he stepped between her parted legs and fumbled at the fastenings of his pants.

'It's the reason I came here, mister!' the woman countered, and faked happy eagerness with the expertise of a whore as she shifted her eyes and head away from Steele to look up at the trooper. And brought up her arms to emphasise her willing readiness.

The the shouting and the laughing rose again, as Joe Harmer, the front of his pants still gaping, crawled on hands and knees to the bottle discarded by Groves. Once in possession of it, he rolled on to his back, sat up and raised the neck to his lips. While Groves dropped hard to his knees and leaned forward to lower himself on to and into the red-headed Gloria. And the rest of the women good-naturedly evaded the more intimate embraces of the men at their sides – urged them and the other troopers to drink up and open fresh bottles.

Then a single shot cracked out.

A pistol shot which might have been mistaken for the crack of a log on the fire. Except for the effect of the shot, which was plainly seen by everyone in the clearing. For the bullet which exploded from the barrel of a revolver aimed from beneath a supply wagon opened up a hole in the centre of Don Groves' forehead; just as the grinning trooper bent his elbows to lower his entire weight on to the woman.

The man became rigid at the moment of his death: and it was Gloria's actions that sent him rolling off her – as she spread her palms, pushed them against his chest and shoved him hard to the side. So that just a few droplets of his blood splashed down on to her face.

A fusillade of gunshots sounded then – to temporarily drown out the shouts which had changed from joy to terror. A half-dozen more troopers suffered fates similar to that of the middle-aged Groves.

Patterson was among them, Jones, too. And young Joe Harmer – hit in the throat as he stared in drunken surprise at the jagged neck of the bottle after a bullet had shattered it.

Gloria powered into a fast roll, as the other women wrenched themselves free of the relaxed grips of the troopers, to drop to the ground or scuttle for cover in crouched runs.

Steele held still for no more than two seconds, watching the carnage with a glint of evil pleasure in his coal black eyes – relishing the punishment his men were taking. Then, as more uniformed figures fell to the trampled grass with dark stains spreading across their tunics or blood gushing from their heads, he struggled to attain some more substantial cover than the shadows beyond the flickering glow of the fire. It was not easy, pushing himself along with his boot heels and the wrists of his bound hands. And as the barrage of gunfire continued, the sweat of fear was added to that of exertion and pain: pasting his clothing to his flesh and running into his eyes and stinging them.

He could no longer see what was happening in the clearing, as he dragged himself around the tree stump and into the brush. But he could hear that fewer men were screaming and cursing and that the shooting was less frantic now – the ambushers able to select, take aim and fire at their targets with calm deliberation. And he breathed a sigh of relief through the fabric of the gag – for he was no longer in danger of being hit by a stray bullet.

A final shot was fired, a body thudded to the ground and Steele became as unmoving as the tree trunks that encircled him: calling himself every kind of fool for enjoying the initial moments of the slaughter and for indulging in the hope that was triggered by a sense of relief. For if every man in his troop was dead – and this was surely inevitable – then he must be destined to go the same way at any moment.

'Careful!' a man rasped. 'Check them over real good! Some of the bastards could be playin' possum.'

Footfalls sounded in the clearing. Gun hammers were cocked. Expended shells were ejected from chambers and fresh bullets were loaded.

'All you women okay?'

'I think I'm gonna be sick,' one of them replied.

A revolver shot cracked.

'This one opened his eyes,' a man drawled in casual explanation.

'Put your threads on, Gloria.'

'That all you can say after all this, Seth?' the redhead muttered.

'You did a good job. All you women did a fine job.'

'Ain't one of the Johnnie Rebs left alive, Seth,' a man reported.

'Then we all did a fine job. Get the horses hitched and let's roll the wagons outa here. You women go on back to town now. We can take care of what's left to do.'

Steele eased his head around, but was unable to see into the clearing through the foliage of the brush into which he had dragged himself. He experienced the threat of nausea again and it was harder to beat this time, as he listened to the activity from a few yards away. Horses snorted and whinnied and their hooves thudded the soft ground. Harnesses and wagon timbers creaked. The flames of the fire hissed and spluttered as they were doused. There was constant talk, but no longer any shouting.

The sensation of total helplessness and the expectation that at any moment he might be remembered and missed kept Steele's stomach churning and his sweat pores open. And time began to play tricks on him again – by turns compressing the minutes to seconds and stretching them to hours just as had happened when he recovered consciousness.

But it was better after he had heard the handcart trundle away and then, a quarter of an hour later, the supply train of wagons roll out of the clearing. And when they had gone from earshot, the timber stand became silent except for the gentle gurgling of the Mississippi flowing among the reeds on the western edge.

Fear drained out of Steele and the sweat dried cold on his flesh. He heard his own breathing and heartbeat. Soon, crickets and bullfrogs and countless other tiny creatures accepted his quiet presence among them and began to move about and voice their calls.

His whole body ached, but the most insistent pain had its centre in the side of his head just back from the top of his right ear. He was mildly grateful for this, since he felt he might have given in to exhaustion had the pain not made sleep impossible.

And there was no time for sleep. The Union army and navy were using the Mississippi to strike deep into the South and it was vitally important to halt the advance. Island Number Ten south of New Madrid Missouri was already in Federal hands and now the Rebels were planning to make a decisive stand at Fort Pillow, which guarded the way to Memphis. But without the ammunition aboard the five wagons which had fallen into enemy hands, the defenders at the fort stood little chance of stemming the waterborne advance.

As Steele struggled out of the brush which snagged at his uniform and scratched his sweating face, he gave no thought to how he might locate the stolen wagons, recapture them and drive them to their intended destination – single-handed. That would come later. First he had to free himself from his bonds.

Clear of the brush and timber, he was forced to rest and, from close to the tree stump where he had watched the mutineers enjoy the rewards of their disloyalty, he surveyed the extent of their punishment. Now that the fire was out there was just the pale moonlight to illuminate the scene, and for the most part he saw the dead troopers as dark lumps on grass. Just here and there a face was turned toward him – a pale blob, sometimes splashed with the darkness of spilled blood.

He made no attempt to try to identify any man, for as individuals they had ceased to exist: and if they should ever need to be remembered, it would simply be as an uncontrollable mob. An awesome example of what men at war could become without the right kind of leadership.

John Patterson was the worst kind of leader. But if Adam Steele had been right, surely the tough waterfront worker from New Orleans would never have been allowed to gain control? Then again, what of the deskbound career army man who had first recommended the Virginia dude as officer material?

Steele shook his head and vented a grunt of disgust through the foul tasting gag. To reflect upon Major Miles Vernon in this context smacked of trying to shed some of the burden of blame for what had happened tonight.

So, as he made slow and awkward progress to the corpse sprawled closest to him, the young lieutenant filled his mind with morose thoughts about Sergeant James Perry. A fine soldier who had narrowly escaped death at Shiloh; only to

44

be gunned down in such cowardly fashion by one of his own men.

'What do you have in mind, mister?' a woman asked.

Her voice struck fear through Steele and he froze, two feet short of the body that was his objective. For a whole second he was unable to move. Then he twisted his head to the side and saw her. The full blown redhead, middle-aged woman who had given herself to young Joe Harmer; then seen Don Groves take a killing bullet in the head as he prepared to enter her. She was dressed now, in a shapeless gown of a pastel shade that hung limply from her shoulders to her ankles. And made small swishing sounds around her legs as she came slowly out of the gap in the trees through which the wagons had been driven.

There was a note of dejection in the way she moved which matched her tone of voice. And when she was close enough for the helpless Steele to see her face clearly, her expression was set in deep lines of remorse.

'A knife, I reckon. But you're wastin' your time, son. The men that done all this took all the weapons off the dead.'

The fear drained out of Steele, only to be replaced by the tension of another emotion – impatience for Gloria to do what she had come back here for.

'The other women, they forgot about you,' she went on after sweeping her sad-eyed gaze over the corpse-littered clearing. 'But I never did. Had to pretend to, though. But I came back first chance I had. It was terrible what we done. Little more than boys, most of you. Didn't realise that until it was too late to stop. Reckon I'm not the only woman feeling bad about it now. Could be why you were forgot about. Got other things on their minds.'

Steele vented a muffled sound through the gag. It was enough to draw her attention to his face, and she made a throaty sound of her own when she saw the tacit request in his eyes.

45

'Oh, I'm sorry.' She hiked up the skirts of her gown, exposing bare legs from ankles to the tops of the thighs. There was a garter encircling the right one, with the handle of a knife protruding from a leather sheath. She drew the knife, and its finely honed blade quickly severed the rope binding his ankles. Then, when he rolled on to his side, she cut the bond on his wrists.

She straightened as he folded up into a sitting posture and dragged the gag away from his mouth.

'I'm real grateful to you, ma'am,' he said huskily, as he massaged feeling back into his numbed wrists.

'It's little enough.' Again she looked around at the dark, inert lumps of the dead men.

Steele gingerly got to his feet, new pain hammering dully in his head, his limbs feeling rubbery and unreliable. 'You could make it more, ma'am.'

'What?'

'Tell me where the wagons were taken?'

'They were still in Attrill when I left to come back here,' she said with a shrug. Then strengthened her tone. 'But you've got no chance of gettin' them back, son. The men are guardin' them. Word's been sent to some bigwig Union officer to come get them.'

Steele interrupted his grimacing efforts to get his circulation working properly to show surprise. 'It wasn't Union soldiers who did this?'

Gloria shook her head. 'No, son. Way it was, a couple of youngsters were out in a boat fishin' when you people made camp here. Come back to town and told their Pas what they'd seen. Attrill folks don't want no part of this war, but they know they're caught up in it. And the way thing's been goin', they figure the Yankees'll capture this piece of the state soon. So they done what they did to keep in good with the Northerners.'

Steele nodded and pursed his lips to exhale a soft sigh.

'Reckon everyone has to do what they can to protect their own at times like these.' As he said this, he recalled the last time he had seen his father and the girl whom he had asked to marry him. It had been at the Chimborazo Hospital in Richmond. After Rich Mountain and before Shiloh. When, had it not been settled before, it was certainly seen to be so then – Ben Steele was committed to support the Union and Diana Summers felt duty bound to side with her father, who subscribed to the same cause as his fellow plantation owners.

'That sure is so, son,' the woman agreed dully. 'And ain't no gettin' away from it – what the women done was real brave. Men gotta be admired, too. They're just ordinary folks. Not trained soldiers. Wasn't that they was hidin' behind women's skirts until it was safe to start shootin'.'

Apart from the nagging pain in his head, Steele felt almost back to normal. Weary and drained, but confident of his ability to reach Attrill without collapsing from exhaustion. 'How was it you were the only one to take her skirt off, ma'am?' he asked, surveying the dead once again and wondering if it was worthwhile checking them to see if any weapons had been overlooked by the ambushers.

'On account of I'm the only one used to it, son,' she answered and for the first time there was power in her eyes. For her gaze challenged him to scorn her as she went on, 'For strangers, anyways. I'm the town whore in Attrill. Just part-time. Run the boardin' house and make myself available to lonely guests.'

The Virginian merely nodded, recalling the expression on her face while she was under the young trooper, and her words of invitation to the much older one.

'If I hadn't agreed to play the part I did – keep your boys amused that way while the men was gettin' close and before any of the other women was forced to do it – well, I reckon none of this would've happened.' Sadness spread across her face again and caused her shoulders to sag. 'Maybe that's the reason I feel so bad about all this.'

'That knife what you carve the supper time meat with?' Steele asked, abandoning the idea of searching the dead for weapons.

She opened her hand and looked down at the knife balanced across the palm. 'Used to be a full-time whore. At a cathouse in Charleston, South Carolina. Kind of customers we used to get there – seafarin' men mostly – a woman sometimes needed to defend herself.'

'Like to buy it off you, ma'am?'

'Dead man's got no need of such!' a voice snarled.

Both Steele and Gloria had to swing into a half-turn to look toward the man who stepped out of the shadows of the wood and into the moonlit clearing. A short, rotund man in his mid-fifties attired in a city-style suit, string tie and derby hat. Right arm thrust out in front of him aiming a small firearm at the couple.

'Damn you, Bill Crease!' the woman growled. 'Why the hell you want to come back here for?'

When the man closed to within twenty feet of him, Steele recognised the gun as a .41 calibre Remington Double Derringer with under and over barrels. Capable of killing instantly over a short range.

'My Bess suddenly remembered about the officer the Rebs made a prisoner of and I come out to take care of him, Gloria,' the man said grimly.

'All on your lonesome!' the woman taunted. 'Because you figured he'd still be tied hand and foot and you could handle him.'

Crease halted ten feet from the couple, scowling in response to the insulting words. 'I can handle him all right now! And you, too. I been in the trees listenin' to every word you told him. Up to you. I can kill you here and now along

48

with him. Or you can come back and face the folks you tried to betray.'

The man had to get closer to make sure of a killing shot and Steele tensed his muscles in readiness – to lunge at Crease and hopefully surprise him into firing wildly. But the man from Attrill showed no sign that he intended to advance further and the gap was too wide. Even over such a range, a lucky shot could strike a killing blow. If not that, open up a disabling wound which would leave the Virginian helpless to combat a second shot from closer.

'Sorry, son,' Gloria murmured in a melancholic tone as she turned her back on Steele. 'I done my best for you, but it seems it wasn't meant to be.'

Hopelessness gripped the Virginian and threatened to drain him of his final reserves of the will to fight. The twin muzzled gun which had hovered between him and the woman now swung to draw a bead on his chest.

'Wise decision, Gloria,' Crease said, his confidence mounting by the split second. 'Just could be the folks in town will overlook this. After you being so much help earlier. Oh . . . '

He had started to smile his triumph. But abruptly the expression changed to a grimace of fear. And he jerked the Derringer to the side, squeezed the trigger a moment after blurting out the exclamation. The knife was spinning through the air then, and in his anxiety to put a bullet into the woman who had hurled it, he was too slow in trying to dodge it.

There had been time and opportunity for Gloria to raise and draw back her throwing arm while Crease was staring at Steele and gloating. So the knife was released from her hand at the end of a powerful forward arc. And when it struck home in the man's chest, left of centre, it had the force to sink three quarters of its blade through his flesh.

Its victim staggered backwards, hurling the gun away, and fell heavily to the ground.

4

Gloria was still on her feet. Was able to whisper, 'Fittin' end, son,' before she too crumpled and corkscrewed to the grass. Blood was blossoming in an ugly stain across the paleness of the dress fabric contouring her left breast. More dark crimson spurted from the bullet hole as she hit the ground, and then the flow was halted, signalling that her punctured heart had ceased to pump.

Selfishly, Steele experienced a pang of pity for the dead woman. For despite her part in the slaughter of his troop, she had saved his life. And it seemed tragic that she should be killed by a lucky shot from the gun of a man whom she had finished with a knife throw of considerable skill.

But then the Virginian banished such irrelevant thoughts from his mind, as he went over to the dead man, stooped, wrenched the knife from the wound and wiped the blade clean of blood on its victim's suit jacket. He had already seen enough of this war to have learned that a man had to make the most of good fortune and do what he could to reverse the bad – at whatever cost. And if there was time to spare for compassion, it was wasted on the dead.

Right now there was no time to spare for anything that did not contribute to the task of reaching the town of Attrill and locating the stolen wagons.

Searching Bill Crease's clothing and finding six loose shells in one of his pockets was a contribution. Another was delving up under the skirts of the dead woman's dress and sliding off the garter with the knife sheath attached. The idea of wearing the knife in a concealed position appealed to him, but not at thigh height. So he twisted the elasticated garter twice until it hugged his calf at the right tension. And after he had used the point of the blade to sever some of the stitches on the outer seam of his right pants legs, he found it simple to delve in through the split and reach the knife.

But as he tested the technique a few times, he had scant

50

hope of ever being such an expert knife thrower as the woman had been. For this was a skill which it had never been necessary for him to develop in the hunting, shooting and fishing which had entertained him during the rich years of peace.

Then he left the clearing, moving between the wheel ruts cut by the stolen wagon and paused at the northern fringe of the timber stand to gaze out across the silent, empty country toward the hill which hid his objective. He felt another pang of grief knife through him when he saw the sprawled, stiffening corpse of James Perry off to one side; then experienced a more acid bitterness as he recalled how his command had sent the non-com to his wasteful death.

But he swept the emotion aside and his voice and expression were grim as he rasped: 'That's the lousy army for you, Sergeant. It was just in the order of things.'

CHAPTER THREE

ATTRILL had started as merely a ferry crossing to over-
come the obstacle of the Mississippi river on the east to
west trail. Steele saw this as he looked down upon the
small community from the cover of a hollow under the
crest on the north side of the rise.

The landing stage, ferryman's house and the two timber
boats at the water's edge all showed signs of age; while the
twin rows of buildings which faced each other across the
broad single street of the town were much newer. And they
were built on higher ground, perhaps safe from the rising
water when the Big Muddy flooded.

It was a farming town, set in rich growing country:
bounded on the south by the hill, the west by the river and
the north and east by an extensive expanse of timber. And
behind the buildings flanking the street, and to either side of
the trail which curved in from the south-east, there was a
patchwork pattern of large fields which cropped cotton,
corn, tobacco and long grass for hay.

The farmers who worked the fields lived in the town, for
there were no homesteads scattered out in the country. And
from where the Virginian looked down upon Attrill, it
seemed that most of the brick and frame buildings lining the
street were small private houses. Only two buildings rose

above single storey and these were on the south side of the street, next door to each other.

The rear of one of the covered wagons was visible at the mouth of the alley which separated the two large buildings from a row of houses. It seemed reasonable to assume that the entire train was parked in front of them on the street.

He spent a full fifteen minutes in the hollow, resting and watching for movement down in the small town: believing what Crease had said about the wagons being under guard, and needing to know how many sentries there were and their positions before making any plan of attack.

He saw one man twice, taking his duty seriously – swinging around the rear of the last wagon in line, a carbine canted to his shoulder. And for several minutes he saw blue tobacco smoke rising through the pale glow of lamp-light that created a ghostly aura above the large building on his left.

There might be others on watch, he realised, as he started cautiously down the slope, but he could not afford to spare any more time in searching for them from a distance. The light of morning was still a long way off, so the dawn of the new day was not his worry. What did make him uneasy was the presence of Bess Crease in one of Attrill's houses.

Gloria had left town secretly and presumably would not be missed until morning. But how long would the wife of Bill Crease remain anxiously silent before telling others of her husband's lone mission?

So, by turns moving in a crouch, crawling on hands and knees, and bellying over the ground, Steele approached the town: aware of the fact that the only person with a reason to expect an intruder from the south could be watching from a window that looked out over the slope.

But he achieved the moon-shadowed back lots of the large buildings without the alarm being raised: muscles aching again and body drenched with sweat in response to high tension. There he dropped to his haunches beside a long, low building that smelled and sounded of horses. Then heard footfalls on a boardwalk. And a voice.

'Still say it's a waste of good sleepin' time, Seth. If any Rebs were gonna come, they'd have been here before now. All that shootin' and all.'

It was the man seated in front of the building with a lighted lamp. Having paused to listen to the growling complaint, the second guard stepped down off the boarding and his footfalls sounded on the hard-packed street as he responded wearily:

'Quit grouchin' Jimmy. After what the womenfolk done to make them soldier boys sittin' ducks, losin' some shuteye is little enough.'

Steele eased his sweat-greasy grip around the butt of the small Derringer and jutted out his lower lip to blow a cooling draught of air up over his face. Then he moved along the front of the stable block to the rear brick wall of the building which seemed to be the town's stage line depot: turning to go through a twenty feet wide gap into the alley, at the mouth of which the rear of the last wagon could be seen. He was able to pull back into the cover of the stone chimney at the side of the building when the guard named Seth made another swing around the wagon and stepped up again on to the sidewalk.

The alley was only partially in moon shadow and he made sure to take advantage of the darkened area – not least because of the sign above a store window directly across the street: *William Crease Grocery*. Both the display window and the glass panel of the door were solid black, but there could well be a chink in one of the blinds through which a worrying woman could be keeping watch.

'Sit awhile why don't you?' Jimmy growled, and struck a match. Just then Steele reached the mouth of the alley.

'You ain't doin' the chore no better than I am by prowlin' up and down.'

'I'm too damn fired up,' Seth answered. And he sounded it. 'I ain't never killed anybody before. I don't know how you can just sit there smokin' the way you are. Or how the rest can just go to bed and sleep. After what was done down in Witch Wood.'

While the man with a troubled conscience was speaking, Steele swept a glance along the street in both directions and looked fractionally longer at the darkened store front opposite. Then he snaked under the two foot high sidewalk, where he rolled over on to his back and used his free hand to drag cobwebs off his face.

Having said his piece, Seth stepped down on to the street again and began yet another circuit of the parked wagons.

From his hurried survey of the street Steele knew that he was indeed under the sidewalk in front of the stage line depot. While next door was the Attrill Hotel, it's jutting sign illuminated from a lamp hung above it. Below and to the left of the sign and lamp was a bench and it was on this that Jimmy was seated, smoking a cheroot.

The line of five covered wagons were parked tight in to the sidewalk, nose to tail with the drawpoles elevated to the vertical position.

When he had glanced eastwards along the short street, Steele's grim-faced attention had been held for a fleeting split second by just one sign. A modest shingle in front of two houses converted to one which proclaimed: *Gloria's – Rooms for Rent*. And he felt mildly pleased that he viewed the home of the dead woman with no more emotion than any other aspect of the small town.

He saw Seth's booted feet beyond the last wagon in the line and watched them as the man rounded the tailgate: cracked his eyes as motes of dust showered down when the man started along the sidewalk.

Both guards were in the same middle-age group as Bill Crease, but they had the burnished complexions and were attired in the denim style of outdoor manual workers. They toted Spencer carbines, which may or may not have been taken from dead troopers.

Steele wondered what the hell he was going to do now that he had got this close to the stolen wagons.

A bell tinkled. A clear, pleasant sound against the footfalls of Seth and the more distant gurgling noises of the Mississippi flowing around the ferry landing stage and the two moored boats.

Seth was now on his second circuit and halted directly above where the Virginian lay – grunted and swung towards the new sound, as the man below him twisted his head to the side to peer in the same direction.

Jimmy gave a short laugh and growled: 'Just the grocery store door is all. Reckon Bill is . . .'

'Mr Haven? Is that you, Mr Haven?'

The woman who emerged from the doorway was hurriedly dressed in a shapeless black gown and her hair was in curlers. So she looked a lot less attractive than when Steele had last seen her – laughing as she allowed herself to be embraced by Trooper Jones while she held a bottle to his mouth.

'And me, Bess. Seth Hubbard. Somethin' wrong?'

She had halted to call her query. Now she hurried across the street and stopped in the mouth of the alley, less than four feet from the Virginian's boots.

'It's Bill, Mr Hubbard,' she started to explain as Haven rose from the bench and came along the sidewalk. 'I told him not to go alone. But he insisted. He was so shamed he never fired a single shot and he insisted. But he's been gone a long time.'

'Gone where?' Haven snapped, no longer sounding bored and weary.

'Back to Witch Wood!' she blurted out.

'What the hell for?' From Hubbard.

'I remembered about the officer . . . about how he tried to send us back to town . . . and . . .'

'Damnit, we only heard about the men killin' their sergeant!' Haven snarled.

'There was a lieutenant,' Hubbard said grimly. 'But Ginny told me he was as dead as the other guy after he got smacked on the head with a gun barrel.'

'No,' Bess Crease countered. 'Or maybe he was. I don't know. But I remember one of the men telling another to tie up the officer. It all happened so fast, the way the soldiers were so eager to get us to the camp. I didn't think about the officer again until Bill and me went to bed. But he's been gone so long, There's been plenty of time for him to . . . '

'Damnit, we gotta go see, Seth,' Haven snapped.

'How long ago, Bess?' Hubbard asked, a lot calmer than the other man. 'Since Bill took off?'

'Two hours at least,' she answered anxiously.

'That's too damn long,' Hubbard growled. 'Why the hell didn't you . . . '

'How'd you mean, Seth?' Haven cut in.

'It should only have took Bill an hour at most,' Bess supplied. 'I know that, Seth. But he so much wanted to handle this on his own. He told me not to . . . '

'You mean he could be in trouble?' Haven asked, a nervous shuffling of his feet matching the nervous tremor in his voice.

'We sure as hell gotta find out one way or the other, Jimmy. Bess, you get back in the store. Jimmy and me'll knock on some doors and take some of the others out to Witch Wood.'

'But I want to . . . ' the woman began, and then allowed her anxious words to trail away as the two men stepped down from the sidewalk – bellowing the names of fellow citizens.

Steele moved a gloved hand, to run the back of it across his brow and wipe off the slick sweat of tension. And did not realise he had been holding his breath until he heard it whistle out between compressed lips, as the woman turned and started back across the street toward the grocery store. But he could have made much more noise in perfect safety, for the once quiet town was now filled with the sounds of raised voices, heavy footfalls and opening doors and windows: as wedges of light from freshly lit lamps stabbed out across the street. And he almost did – felt his mouth open and experienced the threat of an involuntary gust of laughter rise to his throat.

But he checked it.

Hubbard and Haven and the men they were rousing from sleep were not thinking straight: were still in a state of panic after hearing Bess Crease's news. If just one of them paused to consider the many possible ramifications of Bill Crease's long absence, Steele's sense of victory was likely to be a prelude to defeat.

So he watched and listened and waited tensely: more aware than ever of his vulnerability. And experienced a rising anger at himself for getting so close to his objective without first formulating even the basics of a plan to retrieve the stolen supply wagons.

There was less shouting now. And a lull in the activity on the street. But the period of highly charged peace did not last for long – was curtailed when hurriedly dressed men appeared astride their horses.

'All right, all right!' Seth Hubbard yelled, as the riders drew their mounts into a group around him. And women, silhouetted in lighted doorways, peered anxiously out at them. 'Guess you all know why we're up and about. We're gonna ride out to Witch Wood and see if we can find Bill

Crease and the Reb officer so many folks forgot about. What we do when we get there depends on . . . '

'Shouldn't some of us stay here and guard the wagons, Seth?' a man interrupted.

'And the women?' another added.

There were sounds of agreement.

'If the Reb's alive and free, he's just one man!' Hubbard yelled over the noise and silenced it. 'What he'd do is go get some help. Or maybe just take off. Runnin' scared after what happened to his men. And could be that's why Bill is so long gone. Went off after him. No. Witch Wood is gonna take some searchin' and the more of us there are to do the job, quicker it'll be done.'

He turned in the saddle to look along each side of the street: and if he noticed the lack of lighted windows in the façade of the boarding house, he gave no sign of thinking anything of it. 'Ain't no harm in you women keepin' your eyes peeled, though. And after the way you handled yourselves out at Witch Wood earlier, just one Reb soldier won't give you no trouble, I'll bet. Not that he'll be fool enough to come here to Attrill all on his own. Let's go, men!'

He wheeled his horse to the front of the group and heeled the animal forward. The other men, some casting anxious glances toward the women, fell in behind him. And before the group was clear of the street and on the open trail, the horses were up to a dust-raising gallop.

Steele confined the expression of his feelings to a tight grin of satisfaction as the dust settled, the thud of hooves diminished and the soft voices of worried women reached his ears – none of their words clear or loud enough to be understood against the general hum of talk.

He began to move beneath the sidewalk, inching along on his back – head twisted around to watch some of the women emerging from their houses to gather in groups on the street. Peering from under the boarding and through the wheel spokes of the wagons, he could see just the booted feet and lower skirts of the women's dresses. Then he did a double take at one group – and saw the barrel of a carbine and stock of another. Looked at other groups and counted at least half a dozen Spencers.

He moved faster then. As fast as the need for silence allowed. The women unwittingly helping to cover the sounds of his progress with footfalls, as they gathered into a single large group in front of the grocery store.

'That Seth Hubbard, he's so full of his own self importance to my mind,' a woman complained.

'Somebody had to decide what to do,' another countered.

'And it's always him.'

'Ladies, ladies!'

Steele recognised this as the voice of the blonde woman who had done most of the talking when the group was challenged at the fringe of the wood. And she continued to talk now, as the Virginian eased out from under the sidewalk and snaked up on to the boarding, midway along the line of parked wagons. Then rose on to all fours and crawled in through the open doorway beneath the lamplit sign which marked the building as the Attrill Hotel.

'What's done is done. Bess, your man shouldn't have gone off alone the way he did. And maybe Seth Hubbard should've taken account of what some of the others was sayin'. But like he said, we gave a good account of ourselves out at Witch Wood awhile back. And I reckon we can do a good job of guardin' the wagons in case that Rebel officer does show up and try somethin'.'

This claim was greeted with enthusiastic approval, which brought a scowl to the face of Adam Steele as he pulled himself painfully upright in the darkness of the hotel lobby.

'Somebody's missin'!' Bess Crease called out.

'Who's that?'

'Gloria. Where's Gloria?'

There was another hubbub of talk during which every word was drowned by another. Steele crossed the small, spartanly furnished hotel lobby and went up the stairway: his eyes gradually adjusting to the darkness after the lights out on the street.

There were four closed doors along each landing wall and he first went into a room that overlooked the back lot of the hotel: where he eased open a window and looked down at the fifteen foot drop to the hard-packed yard. And scowled again before he left the room, carrying the lamp from the table beside the bedhead. Then he entered each of the street-facing rooms and gathered up the lamps from these: did not look out of any more windows until he was in the final room, with five lamps clutched to his chest in both arms.

He saw that the group of women had now moved along the street and was gathered in front of the boarding house, where one of their number was banging a fist against the door.

'You don't think . . . ' a woman called, as the Virginian eased open a window after setting down the lamps on the floor.

'What are you sayin', Annabelle?' Bess Crease shrieked.

'No, it can't be nothin' like that!' the blonde woman intervened. 'It's common knowledge Bill had no time for Gloria and her ways!'

A tight smile fractionally parted Adam Steele's lips as he realised the women of Attrill were again unintentionally helping him. And further held back from taking any positive action – arguing the merits of the notion that Bill Crease and Gloria had run off together, as the woman at the doorway abandoned her task of banging at the panel and returned to the group. Voices were raised in anger and were counterpointed by plaintive cries of denial from other women. And by the time the blonde had successfully shrieked for silence, all five lamps were burning, filling the small room with the pungent odour of oil. But just a faint glow of light, for the wicks were set to their lowest – a level of light which would not show outside the window which was already bathed in illumination from the lamp above the hotel sign.

Then the time for secrecy was over. And for just a moment Steele experienced a sense of failure: as bitter as that when he saw his troop cut down by the fusillade of gunfire from ambush. For not only had he lost his men. He was now, by his own actions, about to lose the supplies of ammunition which were so vital to the defence of Fort Pillow.

He turned up one of the lamp wicks, rose above the sill level of the open window and hurled the lamp outside. Aiming for the front nearside wheel of the last wagon in the line and venting a grunt of pleasure when he hit it – saw the glass funnel and ceramic base shatter to spray oil along the wagon and the sidewalk.

This was war and he had seen enough of it to know that if victory in a battle was not possible, then it was a soldier's duty to salvage what he could from defeat.

Women's voices were raised louder than ever – in shock, then anger or fear. As all of them whirled to look toward the source of the shattering sounds – and saw one flame become many.

Steele hurled a second flaring lamp at the last but one wagon. It dropped short, was smashed on the sidewalk, but sprayed flaming oil along the length of the wagon. He should have realised at the outset that there had never been any chance of recapturing the wagons and delivering their contents to Fort Pillow. Just one man against an entire town of determined people. So the obvious solution had always been to destroy the supply train to keep the ammunition out of the hands of the enemy.

He tossed a third lamp out of the window. This was not

a battle in strict military terms. He was the only soldier and he was up against a bunch of civilians. Civilians in skirts and bloomers and their curlers. But that was immaterial. These women had been largely responsible for wiping out his entire troop . . .

And as he reflected bitterly on the slaughter he had witnessed in Witch Wood, the women of Attrill provided further evidence of their ability to give more than moral support to the Union cause. For a volley of gunshots cracked out and bullets rushed through leaping flames and broiling smoke to shatter windows and pit the brickwork of the hotel façade.

Steele cursed and hurled himself to the floor as one of the wildly fired shots whined through the open window, showering plaster from the hole it dug in the ceiling.

He heard strident shouts against the crackle of flames, chanced a look out of the window and could see nothing through the thick black smoke. Then, as more shots exploded bullets at the hotel front, he took a greater risk: turned up the wicks of the remaining two lamps and stood to hurl them in quick succession through the window. They were sent in a higher, longer arc than those which had gone before – aimed blind through the thick, black cloud that hid the women from him and him from them.

Seconds later he heard screams of pain or terror or both. And he growled a childish: 'Take that you murdering bitches!' as he whirled, ran out of the room, along the landing and into the open doorway of the room at the rear. Then, as he swung a leg over the sill of the open window, he showed a brutal grin of pleasure as he created a mental image of the Attrill women with their hair and their dresses in flames. But he forced his mind to concentrate entirely on readying himself physically for the impact with the ground, as he launched himself clear of the window.

He hit hard, bent his knees, hunched his shoulders and

tucked his chin down on to his chest as he toppled and rolled. The entire length of his right arm was host to a searing bolt of agony when the elbow cracked against a rusty discarded horseshoe. But he struggled against the need to rest and recover as another vivid image filled his mind – three ammunition laden wagons engulfed in flames, the fire spreading to the other two.

And he rose, stumbled, rose again and began to run. Bullets exploded. But only from the muzzles of carbines, as certain of the women continued to blast wildly at the hotel's upper storey. Soon, though, other bullets would explode. And high explosive shells and mortars. Minor detonations at first, maybe. But building up into a chain reaction, which in combination with the heat of the blazing fire would surely culminate into a massive blast. Destroying everything within a wide radius of its centre.

So Steele ran faster, arcing wide to avoid the dividing fences and outbuildings of the back lots of the houses. Putting the red glow of the fire further behind him and closing the gap on the moon-silvered Mississippi river.

The tiny Double Derringer was clutched in his gloved right hand, and he was aware of the constriction of Gloria's garter around the calf of his right leg. He cursed himself for not having taken the time to search the hotel for a more effective weapon. Then cursed again – aloud – when he saw lights ahead of him. At a window and an open doorway, with a dark figure silhouetted against each patch of yellow.

The house of the ferryman was directly in front of him, isolated from the buildings of the town. He had not forgotten it was there – had simply assumed that its occupants had acted in concert with the other citizens of Attrill. But there was a woman at the window and a man stood on the threshold.

'What in tarnation's happenin'?' the man yelled as Steele neared him.

The Virginian skidded to a breathless halt and felt his whole body aching from the effects of old and new punishments and exertions. But was able to bring up the tiny handgun and aim it at the man who emerged from the doorway, leaning forward in an attitude of concentration.

'No, please don't!' the woman shrieked as she lunged away from the window and out of the door, to drape an arm around the man's shoulders.

He was old and grey haired and wrinkled. She was a quarter his age and pretty. Both of them were dressed in nightwear.

'Grandpa's blind! He can't harm you! He can't do nothin' except get the ferry back and forth across the river! You go. We won't do . . . '

'What's he . . . ' the old man started.

Then both her plea and his question were ended by a small explosion – like a box of July Fourth firecrackers going off at once. And a moment later the five supply wagons were blown to smithereens. Each went up individually, yet in such quick succession it seemed there was just the single detonation.

In the bright flash, Steele saw the sightless stare in the old man's dark eyes: and the paralysing spell which held the girl's gaze fixed upon the scene at the centre of Attrill. And he glanced over his shoulder to see for himself what had terrified her.

For a moment, he saw nothing except blinding light: as he felt the heat of the fire on his sweating flesh and his body buffeted by blast. Then he saw debris begin to rain down, coils of smoke drifting and flames licking upwards. No human being could be seen or heard for what seemed like a very long time. Then, from out of the smoke, a woman appeared: wailing through the hands which she had thrown up to her face. She moved slowly, weaving from side to side. She was naked, the clothing obviously wrenched from her

5

body by the blast. Not burned, and apparently physically unhurt – until she turned to stagger back toward the centre of the devastation. Then it could be seen that a length of iron was buried in her back, with a trickle of blood seeping from the wound and coursing over her flesh.

She halted, let out a final shrill wail and toppled forward: rolled over on to her back, splayed her arms and legs and became still.

'I told 'em, Annie,' the old man said. 'Didn't I tell them, girl? Don't have nothin' to do with this crazy war.'

Annie was still rigid with shock and continued to stare transfixed at Attrill as the smoke of the explosions cleared and other aspects of death and destruction came into view: illuminated by the fires which burned in every building at the centre of town.

'You hear me, girl? You all right?'

She was still clutching the blind old man to her, but was obviously unaware of anything except what she saw perhaps a hundred and fifty yards away.

'She's in shock, mister,' Steele said hoarsely, when he returned his attention to the couple after seeing enough of the bodies strewn on the street and the fire-ravaged houses and business premises. He lowered the Derringer.

The old man nodded and placed his arm around her waist. 'But safe?'

'I'm a Confederate cavalry lieutenant, mister,' the Virginian replied to the implied question. 'No intention of killing anyone unless they're enemies of the Southern cause.'

'I'm nobody's enemy, son,' the blind man said. 'Tried to tell those damn fools in town to be the same. But they wouldn't listen.' He sighed. 'Guess they didn't get you when they pulled that trick down at Witch Wood?'

'That's right.'

'Damn shame, son. About the soldiers gettin' killed. And

the folks you just killed. Was you did the blowin' up, I guess?'

'Sure.'

A shake of the head. 'It's this stinkin' war that's set good people against other good people. Until it got started, don't figure there was anyone in Attrill wouldn't have given a stranger the coat off his back. If it was needed.'

Steele glanced over his shoulder and spread a cynical smile across his face when he saw the raging flames consuming the centre of Attrill. And, just before he witnessed something which altered the smile to a grimace of anguish, he muttered: 'Reckon it sure does look like a warm-hearted town, mister.'

CHAPTER FOUR

THE boy was about seven or eight, dressed in a white nightshirt several sizes too large for him. And as he ran from one sprawled body to another, his legs often became entangled in the fabric and he pitched to the ground. Not until he found the woman he was looking for did he hurl himself down and stay there: embracing the inert flesh and wailing. By which time several other children had emerged from the houses of Attrill and were searching the fire-lit and smoke-layered street.

Steele, grief and remorse etching deep lines into the skin of his youthful face, watched the harrowing scene for stretched seconds – until the intensity of his stare caused it to blur. And he felt himself sway: knew that he might well have collapsed into a faint had not a voice diverted his attention.

'What did you say?' he asked, as he looked again at the old man and the young girl.

'Those poor little mites is what I said,' the girl answered absently. Then filled her voice and her eyes with depthless contempt to add: 'Do they have a special medal for soldiers who make war on women and children?'

'I . . . ' Steele started to reply, but abruptly felt sick to his stomach and pressed his lips together as he struggled to force the bile back down his throat.

'If I was you, son, I wouldn't hang around here too long,' the blind old man advised. 'What happened in town happened loud enough to be heard way beyond Witch Wood.'

Steele beat the nausea, but the threat of fainting from exhaustion was still with him and the scorn which the girl continued to pour on him seemed to have a physical substance that pressed into his body. But he fixed a vivid image of the corpse-littered clearing in his mind and reminded himself firmly how the mothers of the bereaved children had played such a vital part in the slaughter. And for a few seconds he felt a compulsion to voice his thoughts. But he resisted it. The blind old man was right. There was little time to be wasted: and it would certainly be wasted offering lame excuses in the face of the girl's hatred.

'If it bothers you so much, why don't you go see what you can do for the kids,' he snarled.

'And leave my grandfather to your tender mercies!' she flung back at him.

'Do as he says, girl,' the old man urged, and pushed her gently away from him. 'If there is need to kill us, there's nothin' either of us can do to stop him.'

She looked from her grandfather to Steele to the small gun in the gloved hand. And her eyes filled with the tears of terrible helplessness. Then she took a few tentative steps, sneered: 'I'll pray to God you get what's comin' to you!' and broke into a run toward the weeping and wailing children.

'You have a horse here, sir?' Steele asked.

'The girl has. In the stable out back.'

'Grateful to you.'

'Don't be, son. The animal ain't bein' given or loaned to you. You're takin' him. Called stealin'. But after what you done tonight . . . well, normal crimes men commit don't seem like very much.'

There was no contempt or hatred in the blind old man's expression or voice. Only resignation. And that was how Lieutenant Adam Steele came to view the incident in retrospect, as he rode the stolen grey gelding northwards away from Attrill.

For a long time, as he made cautious progress along the eastern bank of the Mississippi, he did not reflect upon the past at all: confining his thoughts to the present and the danger of pursuit. But no one was following him and when he was sure of this he increased his pace as the night sky lightened toward dawn. And then he concerned himself with the future – specifically the situation at Fort Pillow and what effect the non-arrival of the supply train would have on it.

Just for a while, as he rested himself and the gelding between a canebrake and the river, gazing out across the reflection of sunrise on the placid water, he thought back to the sight which had caused him so much anguish – and realised that his subconscious must have been concerned with the subject all along. For the only pain he experienced on this warm and peaceful morning was physical. He had done what he felt he had to do and had collected some bruises in the process . . . but no lasting scars on his mind.

He got wearily to his feet and raked his eyes around as he stroked the nose of the gelding, listening to the rippling water and the gentle sounds of riverside wildlife. And knew he was in a time out of time. In many other parts of this country people were dying and killing – or getting ready to die or kill. That was a fact of war. It was inescapable and therefore had to be accepted. And if a man did not have a death wish, he must kill to survive. If he had any human feeling for his fellow man, he would inevitably experience some degree of regret. But he could not burden himself too heavily or too long with such emotions. For surely he would lose his reason.

70

Steele nodded his acceptance of this and swung up into the saddle: started northwards again to resolutely complete the mission he had set himself. But Fort Pillow was still many hours ride away when a rumble of artillery fire caused him to rein the gelding to a halt. It was mid-morning and he was once more in woodland, shaded from the glare and heat of the sun by the late spring foliage that covered the terrain on the inside of a sweeping bend in the river.

His mount was made skittish by the sound of distant gunfire, perhaps recalling the fear he had experienced during the explosions in Attrill. Steel had calmed the animal then and now he did so again, whispering soothing words into a pricked ear as he himself listened to get a bearing on the direction from which the sound of the shelling came. But the encircling trees acted to subdue and distort the barrage, and once the horse was quiet and obedient again the Virginian angled away from his previous course.

Earlier on, he had been forced to veer away from the river by the trees and tangled brush that spread right to the water's edge. Now he made his way to the bank again – and had to hitch the gelding to a branch and cover the final three hundred feet on foot: grunting and cursing as he forced a passage through fabric-snagging and skin-tearing thorned bushes. So that when he finally saw the sparkling surface of the Mississippi again there was blood as well as sweat smearing his flesh.

The heavy guns continued to fire and his own breathing was loud in his ears. And it was his sense of smell that caused him to pause, draw the tiny Derringer from his tunic pocket and listen for other sounds. For there was smoke in the air. Not the acrid taint of exploded black powder, though. Instead, the much more pleasant aroma of woodsmoke. Not from a house chimney or a campfire. From the stack of a riverboat – the ram prow of which he saw just a moment after he had recognised the engine sound for what it was.

Just as Steele reached the water's edge, crouching low to stay in the cover of the brush, the thud of the engine slowed and the speed of the boat through the water lessened. Chains rattled and an anchor splashed downwards, the iron bit into the riverbed and the forward momentum of the craft was halted. But currents caused her to drift around on the axis of her anchor chain, and in less than three minutes she had completed a one hundred and eighty degree turn and was held almost inert facing upriver: the Confederate States flag hanging limp from her stern mast.

Her name was *Pride of Memphis*, just visible in faded lettering along each side of her superstructure – but she looked anything but proud in her present condition and circumstances. She was a twin stacked sternwheeler, hastily converted for war use as an armed ram ship. Maybe two hundred feet long and broad of beam, probably lower in the water than was safe because of the iron plating that had been rivetted to her hull, decking and superstructure.

She looked ugly and powerful, and yet showed many signs that she was not invulnerable – her armour plating dented, scorched and holed in many areas and her menacing-looking ram sheered off dangerously close to her prow.

Seconds passed after she had come to rest some fifty yards or so from where Steele crouched in the brush, and there was no sign of life aboard the *Pride of Memphis*: her engine idled, smoke drifted lazily from her midships stacks and her wheel turned freely to the dictates of the river currents. Then a group of grey clad figures emerged on to the aft deck, the clatter of their booted feet on plating muffling the words of shouted orders. But the soldiers at whom the commands were directed heard them and they worked fast to man-handle a longboat from under a protective shelter, fix it to davits and lower it into the river. A dozen men clambered down into the boat and axes were thrown to them. Then, with a lieutenant at the tiller, the men pulled for the shore –

72

heading for a stretch of bank several yards upriver from where Steele watched.

With the lieutenant pacing the strokes in a loud, anxious voice, the longboat cut fast through the water and within moments of reaching the bank the sounds of axes biting into timber added an urgent counterpoint to the distant rumbling of the artillery barrage.

Steele rose then, and was not aware of how bone-deep weary he was until his body protested at the demand for further movement after such a short rest. He considered cupping his gloved hands to his mouth and announcing his presence to the men aboard the ironclad or the timber-felling shore party: but resisted the impulse. For he had heard the nervousness in the lieutenant's voice and seen the haggard, pale faces of the officer and the men on the oars. The boat had taken a battering and so had the crew. And the speed of events after the anchor was dropped suggested that the men would feel no lessening of tension until after the *Pride of Memphis* had taken aboard fresh cordwood to fuel her boilers. Men in such a state of mind were likely to consider all strangers enemies, and to shoot before asking questions.

So the Virginian returned to his horse and led him through the wood in the direction from which the sounds of tree felling came. Once again, he had to tether the animal to a branch and suffer more tears in his skin and rents in his uniform as he forced a way through thorn-infested brush. But on this occasion he did not have to sweat and bleed all the way to the river-bank. For the men from the ironclad had landed in a semi-circular clearing which, at its widest point, extended some twenty yards in from the water's edge.

It was on the northern fringe of the clearing that the men were at work – stripped to undershirts or bare-chested, some felling trees, other lopping and logging the fallen trunks and the lieutenant and a corporal stacking the cordwood in the longboat.

'Good morning, Lieutenant!' Steele yelled. And realised it was an inappropriate greeting – but then how else was he to announce he was there?

All but one man stopped what he was doing and whirled toward the newcomer. Some continued to grip axes, but in the attitude of weapons rather than tools. Others replaced them with carbines. While the lieutenant half-drew a revolver from his holster.

Steele had his arms at his sides and slightly forwards, fingers splayed. Now he raised them up to shoulder height. Said quickly: 'I'm alone and we're on the same side.'

'Quit it, O'Brian!' the lieutenant snapped, and the enlisted man who had been putting his all into logging only now became aware of the situation.

'Who the frig are you?' he asked.

Steele continued to advance on the soldiers until he was ten feet away from the anxious lieutenant. 'Steele. Cavalry lieutenant. Attached to the command of General Beauregard. Out of Memphis and headed for Fort Pillow.'

'Don't friggin' bother, mister!' a powerfully built man with a bloodstained bandage around his head growled. 'By the time you reach there it'll be a pile of friggin' rubble with bluebellies crowin' on top of it.'

'Lieutenant Crennell, what's the damn hold up?' a man roared from the ironclad.

'Get back to it, men!' the lanky, thin-faced, blond-haired Crennell ordered. Then cupped his hands around his mouth to respond to the question: 'Company, Major! One man! A CSA cavalry lieutenant! Bound for Pillow!'

'I want to see him aboard this hulk, Lieutenant!'

'Sir! I'll send him out with the first batch of logs!'

'If he thinks he can be of any damn use at Pillow he

ought to be able to walk on the water out here! Hurry up with the damn timber, Crennell!'

Steele gazed at the ironclad during the exchange, but saw the major as just a shadowy figure at one of the gun-ports. Then the work of refuelling the *Pride of Memphis* recommenced, the lieutenant – who was about the same age as Steele – talking as he caught logs thrown by the corporal and stacking them evenly in the longboat.

'The fort's all but had it, Mr Steele. Going to go the same way as Island Number Ten up on the Missouri border. Our so-called River Defence Fleet is no match for the Union's Western Flotilla. For three full weeks their ironclads and mortar boats gave us hell up there. And now you can hear the bastards are using the same tactics at Pillow.' He straightened up from his chore and massaged the small of his back. 'All right, Corporal Dickson. She won't take much more without floundering. You, Cross, Morris and Lieutenant Steele take the oars. Rest of you men keep at it.'

Looking at the men's gaunt, sweat-dripping, bristled and dirt-streaked faces, Steele realised that his weariness was nothing compared with theirs. And he took his place at an oar beside the corporal without complaint: did the best he could at the unaccustomed chore of rowing a boat. While Crennell continued to talk from his position at the tiller – apparently using the outpouring of bitter words as some kind of tension-easing therapy.

'There were eight CSA ironclads up at Pillow a few days ago. Giving hell to the Union mortar boats. Until the Yankees floated in some big bastards. Cut our boys to pieces with shell fire before we could get close enough to use the rams. Nothing else we could do but turn and run. Short of staying there like sitting ducks and have the Yanks send us to the bottom.'

'But we're gonna get our own back, sir,' Dickson put in when Crennell paused for breath. 'The Major has this great idea and when we hit the friggin' bluebellies they'll wish the hell they had never tangled with the *Pride of Memphis*.'

The corporal looked no older than twenty. Short, but stockily built. With bright red hair and a round, pleasant face still troubled by adolescent acne. His blue eyes were bright with excitement as he relished the prospects he spoke of and he even drooled a little – the spittle running through the fuzz on his jaw to drop on to his hairless chest.

'Rest the oars, men!' Crennell ordered, and pushed the tiller hard over, so that the longboat made a graceful turn and slid in smoothly alongside the ironclad.

Then he threw up one line while Dickson scrambled to the bow and hurled another. Both of them were deftly caught and secured. And hands were reached down.

'Compliments of Major Garner, sir. He'd be pleased to see you in his quarters right away.'

Steele was hauled up on to the aft deck of the ironclad, and the moment he was ushered away from the rail by a soldier in an oil and grease-stained undershirt, logs began to be hurled up from the longboat.

'Best if I lead the way, sir,' the man suggested as they moved out of the bright, fresh sunshine of morning and through a companionway into the fetid murk beyond. But because of the light which entered through the gunports and shell holes, Steele's eyes adjusted immediately to the change. And he saw the extent to which the former riverboat had been converted for war.

In this section of the *Pride of Memphis*, which extended from twenty feet back from the bow to ten ahead of the sternwheel, she had been gutted. And except for the lower sections of the two smokestacks and the firebox and boilers between, the area was simply a gun platform armed with twelve pounder howitzers with the field wheels chained to the decking – four along each side and two at the forward end. These two, plus two on the port side, had been damaged: three of them beyond repair.

Four men were engaged in cannibalising the useless howitzers to try to salvage the least badly smashed one – working as hard and sweating as freely as the soldiers who were refuelling the *Pride of Memphis*. And they spared but a glance for the cavalry lieutenant, as Steele was led along the gun deck and up a ladder which canted upwards forward of the boilers. While the newcomer took careful note of everything he saw – from the haunted, terror-filled eyes of the youngest man working on the damaged gun to the many patches of dried blood on the decking. His nostrils drew in the smells of burning wood, hot metal, sweat, human waste and river.

Then he emerged through a hatch into the wheelhouse above the gun deck, blinked in the bright sunlight and breathed deeply of the fresh air pleasantly tinged with woodsmoke that now did no more than wisp from the twin stacks.

'Welcome aboard the *Pride of Memphis*, Mr Steele,' a man greeted dully. 'Major Conrad Garner in command. All right, soldier, return to your assignment. And tell every work detail that unless they double their damn efforts I'll have the whole frigging lot of them transferred to the stinking navy!'

'Sir!' Steele's escort snapped, and whirled around, to slide rather than climb back down the ladder. And for a few moments he could be heard relaying the major's warning to the gun repair crew – until Garner lashed out a foot to slam the hatch shut. And glared with wild eyes at the Virginian as he snarled:

'Soldiers we are, mister! Louisiana Volunteers! Joined the army to fight the frigging Yankees on the ground! Man to man! This is damn navy work!' He spat a stream of dark brown tobacco juice at the already heavily stained deck.

'One officer riding for Fort Pillow? You have a despatch for the command there?'

Garner was a short, solidly built and rigidly erect officer with a round and florid face set with bright button eyes which were green in colour. Although fully dressed in regulation uniform, he was as dishevelled, unshaven and dirty as his men – and as Steele. For the most part he looked close to exhaustion, but his voice was strong and in his staring eyes and his quick, precise movements there was more than a suggestion that he was a lot younger than the fifty odd years he appeared to be – and that he had a vast reserve of energy to call upon if need be.

'In a manner of speaking, sir,' Steele answered, beginning to let his shoulders sag and his arms become limp at his sides. 'When we left Memphis . . .'

'Stay to attention until I tell you otherwise, mister!' Garner cut in harshly. 'Maybe in the smart ass cavalry that's not necessary in the presence of a senior officer! But you're in the real army now! Even if it don't seem that way aboard this sonofabitching hulk!'

Steele pulled himself to ramrod stiffness, compressed his lips and stared straight ahead – over the big helm wheel and out through a slitted aperture at a restricted view of the bend in the river.

'That's a damn sight better, mister,' Garner allowed and walked back and forth in front of the lieutenant a few times, jaws working with clicking sounds as he chewed tobacco. Then he halted immediately in front of Steele, spat juice from the side of his mouth and demanded: 'Now, report.'

The Virginian ached from head to toe as the anger of hatred for the wild-eyed major allied with the strain of rigidly controlled muscles acted to create fresh pain from earlier suffering. 'Yes, sir,' he said tightly. 'I was in command of a troop of men detailed to take a supply train from Memphis to Fort Pillow. Last night we were ambushed, my

78

men were killed and the wagons were stolen. I found the wagons, sir. There was no means to recapture them, so I destroyed them. I now consider it my duty to warn the command at the fort that the expected supplies will not arrive.'

Garner swung around to put his back to Steele and stare out at the bend in the river.

'Born under a lucky star, were you, mister?' he asked grimly.

'Sir?'

'Lost all your men and kept yourself alive?'

Steele felt the flesh of his face being forced into the set of a scowl: but managed to become impassive again as the major whirled round to stare at him.

'Sir, I'm prepared to give a full report of the incident if required. But I consider it more important right now to reach Fort Pillow. They're expecting five wagonloads of ammunition and . . . '

'Ammunition?' Garner snarled.

'Yes, sir. For small arms and artillery. And maybe if . . . '

'Listen, mister!'

Steele struggled to keep his temper in check while he waited for the major to hurl more angry words in his face. But Garner's tone of voice was suddenly lacking in emotion when he said:

'Not to me, Lieutenant. To that din upriver.'

And for a long moment, both men were silent as the wheelhouse was invaded by the sounds from outside. Metal on metal from the gun deck below, the voices of men stowing cordwood in the engine room, the thud of axes against timber on the starboard bank, the gurgling of water along the hull – and the incessant thuds, thumps, whistlings and crashes of the large-scale artillery barrage much further away.

'The boys at the fort are taking hell, mister,' Garner went

79

on in the same toneless voice. 'Sticking it out because Pillow is all that stands between the frigging Yankees and Memphis. No way we can tell from here how many of them shells are being aimed at the fort and how many are coming out of it. But I reckon we can make a good guess that our boys can't afford to waste what they got left. Wouldn't you say, mister?'

'Sir, if I can get to the fort and make my report . . .'

'Report, Lieutenant!' Garner bellowed, cheeks trembling, face getting redder and tobacco juice spraying. 'Listen, man! I told you to listen! Them boys have got Yankee artillery barrels sticking down their throats! And that doesn't leave them any time to listen to lame excuses from some smart ass horsesoldier who hasn't got through with what they want! I've been there, mister. And I lost half my men. Would have stayed and sacrificed everything if needs be. But I was ordered downriver. To take up a rearguard position.'

His eyes dulled, his words lost force and as he began to move back and forth across the wheelhouse again there was a weariness close to despair in his gait.

'Forget Fort Pillow, mister. It's finished. Dead . . . but just won't lay down until every man defending it is dead. The boys up there are doing a fine job. Longer they can hold out, more Yankees they'll kill and the more time Beauregard will have to launch a counter-attack. So forget Pillow, Lieutenant. If the command there learns it will get no fresh supplies, it's likely a withdrawal will be ordered. Which would serve no good purpose. You will stay here, Mr Steele. Under my command. And serve the cause by fighting alongside the other officers and men of the *Pride of Memphis*.' He raised an arm and pointed out through the slit in the wheelhouse's armour plating. 'When we engage as many Union vessels as come around the bend in the river. Until then, you will make yourself available to Lieutenant Crennell and undertake whatever tasks he sees fit to give you. Dismiss, mister!'

Major Garner dropped his arm to his side, but continued to stare out over the damaged ram at the boat's prow at the point where the sparkling river curved from sight among the woods. And for a few seconds Steele was in danger of losing control of his temper – knew that if the senior officer should glance back at him he would see in the younger man's face the struggle that was taking place in his mind. But Garner did not look at Steele as he said grimly:

'I gave you an order, Lieutenant. Follow it at once or I'll have you thrown in the brig.'

The Virginian did not trust himself to speak a single word of acknowledgement without revealing his feelings. So he merely threw up a hasty salute, raised the hatch and climbed down the ladder: felt his features form into a silent snarl of rage when Garner slammed the hatch closed two feet above his head.

'Regular bear with a sore head, ain't he Lieutenant?' one of the men working on the damaged howitzer said with soft-voice sourness.

Steele was on the point of voicing cynical agreement with the soldier. But checked the impulse. Instead remained silent until he stepped off the ladder, by which time his hot temper had been reduced to a hard ball of ice-cold anger held in the pit of his stomach.

'You say something to me, soldier?' he asked, expression still grim but his voice even.

All four men turned their sweat-dripping faces towards him and the mirthless grins died before the levelness of his cold-eyed gaze. Then the man who had spoken swallowed hard and growled: 'Just tryin' to be friendly, sir.'

'Why, feller? You have cause to like me?'

The man swallowed again, confused by the response.

'Aw, the hell with it, O'Toole,' another of the men growled as he crouched to continue with his work, and lowered his voice to rasp: 'Ain't you ever gonna learn that they're all the same – far as guys like us are concerned.'

Steele swung around and went aft, but his footfalls on the decking did not mask the muttered words:

'Yeah, O'Toole. They're all assholes and assholes don't know nothin' else but shittin' on what's under them.'

The Virginian compressed his lips and gritted his teeth: kept on walking at a measured pace until he paused on the threshold between the gun and the aft decks. Where he began to regret his reaction to the men at the damaged gun – the way in which he had unburdened a part of his anger towards Garner on to them. But then, with a sigh, he acknowledged to himself that his attitude had been the right one, albeit impulsively based upon a poor foundation.

For whether an officer was a shavetail lieutenant or a general with many years of combat experience behind him in time of war he had to maintain a gulf between himself and the men. Because how could a man worthy of the term issue an order which was likely to get a friend killed? The way Sergeant James Perry had been shot down.

But surely there was a happy medium between currying favour with the men and the antagonistic tyranny with which Major Garner asserted his authority? And how long would it take Lieutenant Adam Steele to reach it?

'You goin' back ashore now, sir?' the red-haired Corporal Dickson asked from the rail where he was watching the empty longboat being rowed towards the bank, having changed from loading to off-loading duty. 'Have to wait awhile.'

'No, Corporal. I seem to have been pressed into the navy.'

Dickson grinned. 'Glad to have you aboard, sir. And you'll be glad to be with us when the bluebellies show up and the Major gives the bastards what they got comin'.'

One of the other men in the unloading detail spat pointedly into the river when Dickson mentioned the boat's commanding officer. And the non-com glared malevolently at the culprit, then shook his head as he returned his bright blue eyes to Steele.

'Don't pay any attention to what others say about the Major, sir,' he urged. 'He's hard and he's mean, but that's how a good officer oughta be. All man.'

'Grateful for the advice, Corporal,' Steele replied, mildly intrigued by Dickson's glowing praise for Garner as he noted the sneers of contempt which came and went across the faces of the four other men in the detail. 'I was beginning to think everyone aboard regarded Major Garner as just part of a man.'

CHAPTER FIVE

WHEN the fuel store of the *Pride of Memphis* was restocked the three officers and twenty man crew of the riverboat ate a meal of greasy lamb stew and stale bread. Everyone had the food at his assigned duty position or, if he was not on watch, in his rest quarters.

Steele was on watch from midday to three-thirty in the hot, still afternoon – apologetically assigned by Lieutenant Crennell to supervising the details who worked at repairing those areas of damage which did not require the specialised skills and tools of the shipwright. Which simply meant that he constantly patrolled the riverboat from stem to stern and back again – never needing to demand extra effort from the men for they were working flat out, all of them aware that their lives could well depend upon completing the various chores before the expected Union vessels steamed into sight.

If there was talk among the men it was always cut short before he came within earshot and for his part, Steele asked no questions. He was so tired that his ears buzzed and his eyes felt filled with grit. He had to concentrate hard to keep walking in a straight line and before half his watch was over his jaw ached from yawning. At the start he had wondered how the off duty men could sleep through the continuous racket of hammers against metal which all but drowned out the distant thunder of gunfire. But then he realised that in his and their state of exhaustion, it would be easy.

He thought of Virginia. Of the Steele Plantation. Of his father. Diana Summers. Of Jim Bishop, Cornell Banning, Brewster Davidson and other friends from home. Of Cliff Gordon who was not a friend.

Love and hate. Privilege and want. Ecstasy and despair.

'Time to switch with Mr Crennell, sir.'

The Virginian was below decks forward, having checked on the progress of two men who were strengthening the ram supports. And was moving almost trance-like along a companionway with the crew's quarters on one side and the officers' cabins on the other. The voice startled him and he spun around with a small gasp of surprise: saw it was the freshly washed up and now fully dressed Dickson who had spoken, as the corporal emerged from the cabin of Major Garner and closed the door behind him.

'Corporal?'

'Change of watch, sir. That's the door to Mr Crennell's quarters. You can have any of the other quarters, I guess. We lost the captain and two other lieutenants at Pillow.'

'Grateful to you,' Steele said.

'Pleasure, sir,' came the reply, before Dickson squeezed by the Virginian and started up the steps at the end of the companionway, whistling cheerfully.

Steele went to Crennell's door, banged a gloved fist on it and entered without waiting for a reply – which he probably would not have got unless he had kept on knocking for several hours. For inside the narrow, cramped cabin with its single bunk, small bureau and tiny porthole he had to shake the sleeping man violently by the shoulders to rouse him. And even when Crennell was awake, he grunted and groaned and mumbled for long seconds before he realised where he was and who it was who had brought him back to unwelcome reality.

'Something happening?' he asked, as he threw off the single blanket and got groggily to his feet, fully dressed except for his hat.

'Just the time for you to drift around this boat while I get some sleep, feller.'

'Shit, I was hoping the Union Navy would hit us and kill me while I was out,' Crennell growled as he went to the bureau, raised a pitcher from a basin and poured water over his head.

'I hear that kind of talk again from you, mister, and you'll get killed sure enough!' Garner snarled from the companionway as he glared into the cabin. 'By a damn firing squad! On account of that's treason you're talking, mister. Anything to report, Lieutenant Steele?'

'No, sir.'

The major headed in the wake of Dickson and Crennell waited until his footfalls sounded on the stairway before he growled: 'I bet you're real happy you joined, mister.'

He used his bed blanket to soak up the water from his hair and face and emerged from under it looking little better than when he had staggered to his quarters more than three hours earlier: the flesh of his face deathly pale between the stubble and the black half-circles under his eyes.

'Seems the only man who's that is Dickson, feller.'

Crennell was peering into a piece broken mirror, rasping a hand over his jaw as if considering a shave. But then he scowled, snorted and jammed his hat on his head as he swung toward the doorway. 'That's because the sonofabitch is teacher's pet,' he hissed. 'And gets special privileges for special services . . . if you know what I mean?'

Steele was leaning against the doorframe, almost asleep on his feet: blocking the man's exit from the cabin. He did know what Crennell meant, for in the whorehouse of Keysville Virginia which he had often visited during his youth there had been a handsome European boy who provided such special services. And one drunken night Steele and some of his friends – the fat Nick Kane, the squint-eyed Conrad Shotter and the quiet-mannered Andrew Harding, as he recalled – had burst into the back room where the boy worked. To find him working. Kneeling at the foot of the bed, across which was spread-eagled the naked body of a man they all knew. Steele had managed to stagger downstairs and out into a rear alley before throwing up.

'Crennell!' Major Garner bellowed from above. 'Get yourself topside at the double, mister!'

'Topside I don't mind,' the thin-faced and lanky lieutenant muttered with a sour grin. 'I'll kick, though, if ever he orders me to the backside.'

The Virginian started to smile, but it was curtailed by an involuntary yawn as he shifted out of the doorway.

'Sleep well, mister,' Crennell said as he stepped out of the cabin. 'It'll only seem like a couple of frigging seconds.'

He was right.

Steele remembered, as if recalling a fragment of a dream, moving along the companionway, pushing open a door, seeing a replica of Crennell's quarters and closing the door behind him. He had no memory of sprawling out on the narrow bunk, of closing eyes and of the clatter aboard the boat and the rumble of distant gunfire fading from his ears.

'Up, sir! Get up, sir, sir! It's startin' again! The Yankees are comin', sir!'

He forced up his leaden eyelids and saw a vaguely familiar face which did not come into clear focus until the man stopped shaking his shoulders. Then he recognised the man with the bloodstained bandage on his head who had been felling trees earlier. And once this certainty was established in his mind, he recalled everything else that had happened to bring him to this cramped, oven-heated, rancid smelling place.

'Two gunboats steaming downriver, sir,' the soldier reported as he straightened up, less frantically anxious now that Steele was awake. 'And we got us an audience would you believe? Crazy bastards. Major orders every man topside, sir.'

He swung around and went out of the cabin, footfalls sounding at a run along the companionway.

A couple of seconds, Crennell had said. It must have been longer. The heavy weight of unplacated exhaustion caused Steele greater difficulty than old pain as he struggled to sit up, put his feet on the floor and rise. There was a china pitcher and basin, but no water and Steele hurled the pitcher against the wall with a curse, as the stink of sweat on his unwashed flesh erupted the sour taste of bile into his throat.

Then, once the sound of shattering china faded, he became aware of the relative quietness clamped over the ironclad. There was no more hammering and the bombardment of Fort Pillow had ceased. Now there was just the gurgling and sucking of water along the hull and the regular, subdued thud of an idling engine. With, from time to time, the sound of voices and footfalls on the gundeck overhead.

'Mr Steele! You're not in the smart ass cavalry now, mister! When I say turn out, I mean turn out, damnit!'

Scowling his hatred for Garner and with his lips moving to form unspoken obscenities, Steele lurched out of the cabin and ran along the companionway, up the steps and out through a hatch to emerge on the aft deck. Saw from the position of the sun in the western sky that events had not allowed him to take his scheduled three and a half hour rest – that it was only about five o'clock.

'Up here with me, mister!' the major bellowed. 'This is no time to admire the damn view!'

Steele had not paused for more than a second to check the time and relish the fresh river air flowing across his sweat-sheened, heavily bristled face. Now he forced his features into an impassive set and kept his lips pressed firmly together, as he moved into the gloom of the armour plated gun deck. In time to see the florid face of Garner, sideways on, just before the man straightened up to go from sight in the wheelhouse.

But other men watched him as he took long strides towards the ladder beyond the boiler and smokestacks. The men who stood, two to a gun, at each of the starboard and forward placed howitzers. All of them with red rimmed eyes, hollow cheeks, unshaven and dirt-streaked faces. All now in full uniform with sidearms in unfastened holsters. And all with Spencer carbines – bayonets fixed – close at hand: leaning against the guns or on the deck beside the neatly stacked shells.

The Virginian recognised O'Brian from the tree-felling detail and as the man with the bandaged head who had roused him a few moments ago. Cross and Morris who had crewed the longboat with Dickson, Crennel and himself when he came aboard the *Pride of Memphis*. The young soldier whom he had bawled out for expressing sympathy following the humiliating interview with Garner. And the acned Corporal Dickson who was standing at the foot of the ladder to the wheelhouse. He had probably seen every other man, but their faces did not register in his memory – merely fleeting impressions of their expressions as they saw him hurry to comply with the major's command.

Sympathy and pity. Dismay and indifference. Animosity and outright hatred. And underlying what was on the surface of each weary face was some degree of fear. Selfish fear.

A sole exception was Dickson, who was grinning like an excited child promised a special treat.

'We'll show 'em, sir, won't we?' he said eagerly as Steele started up the ladder, 'we'll make them bluebellies wish they'd stayed up in their own lousy country!'

Steele glanced down at the youthful face and saw that the eyes were as bright as ever, the mouth was gaping open to

89

emphasise the degree of near ecstatic excitement that Dickson was enjoying. And abruptly his exhaustion-addled mind conjured up a vivid image of what the boy had been doing to the man in the back room of the Keysville whorehouse.

Fresh bile rose into his throat and he wrenched his gaze away from Dickson's face and tried to mask his retching by a forced fit of coughing, as he staggered up into the wheelhouse. But Major Garner, who whirled away from the slitted aperture directly in front of the helm saw through the subterfuge: misjudged the cause of the Virginian's threatened nausea.

'So that's why you wanted away from this boat soon as you knew we expected trouble, mister!' the major roared.

'Sir?' Steele asked, puzzled.

'Because you knew you'd want to throw up at the first sight of the enemy!' Garner spat so forcefully that the plug of tobacco was ejected from his mouth with a stream of juice. 'Goddamn you high-nosed cavalry officers . . . snotnosed sons of rich men . . . yellow clean through from your bellies to your backbones – if you had any friggin' backbones!'

Steele suddenly did not feel in the least tired. For, as he locked his stare on the deeply coloured face of the ranting major and heard his shrill accusations ringing in his ears, he felt an uncontrollable urge to lunge at the man, put his hands around the thick neck and squeeze. And imbedded deep in his mind was the undeniable belief that he could succeed in satiating this desire that was stronger than any he had ever experienced before.

But then, a fraction of a second before he submitted to the impulse, the scene in the clearing on the bank caught his eye. It was too late to hold back from the physical action his mind had demanded. And he went forward – knew from the look of terror on Garner's face as the major threw himself sideways that the officer had seen Steele's initial intention in the set of his expression. But the Virginian's plan had changed. Instead of the man, it was his position at the aperture that Steele sought. And when he reached it, he stood stock-still, staring out at the clearing which had been enlarged by tree felling.

There were upwards of a hundred people aligned along the bank, the number swelling by the minute as others ran through openings in the brush created by the first to arrive. Men, women and some children of all ages and sizes: and all social levels judging by the variety of their dress.

And we got us an audience would you believe? While Steele raked his coal-black eyes over the gathering throng, he recalled the words the man with the bandaged head had yelled at him after waking him in the cabin. Then he re-membered other words: spoken to him by his father at the hospital in Richmond. When Ben Steele had told him how the rich of Washington had ridden out with picnic hampers to watch the Bull Run battle as if it was some carefully staged pageant.

Bull Run? No, that was what the Union called it and Ben Steele supported the Yankees. Adam Steele was a Con-federate and to the South it was the Battle of Manassas Junction.

But names didn't matter. It was all crazy. There was a terrible and bloody war splitting the country apart. And people were too stupid to realise it. Brought their families out of the safety of their own homes to watch men kill each other.

Had the children of Attrill been so safe in their own homes last night when Steele exploded the supply wagons . . ?

'What's the damn matter, mister? You too shit scared to move a muscle now? Corporal, get up here! Cross, take Dickson's place!'

'Sir!'

'Yes, sir!'

Dickson's footfalls on the ladder accompanied the

acknowledgement of the orders. Steele slowly turned away from the slit in the iron plating, his mind clearing of superfluous memories and his weary eyes noting the tell-tale black smoke in the sky above the trees beyond the bend in the river.

'Listen, you loud mouth bastard,' he rasped through teeth clenched between curled back lips. 'You've got a fight on your hands and a whole bunch of men whose lives depend on how you handle it!'

'Don't you try to tell me my duty, you jumped up little . . .'

Dickson's head and shoulders appeared in the hatchway and Steele cut in on Garner's snarling words to snap, 'Get back to your post, Corporal! And tell Cross to do the same!'

'Sir?' Dickson pleaded to the major.

'I'm in command . . .'

'So give me the order you had in mind when you had me come up here,' Steele said levelly. 'And shoot off your mouth in a report about my conduct if any of us get out of this alive.'

Garner was all but consumed with rage, shaking from head to foot, saliva running out over his trembling lower lip. Sweat beaded every pore on his crimson face.

'Hey, you guys!' a man roared clearly from the bank. 'They're here! The lousy Yanks are almost here! Give them the works, uh?'

A cheer greeted the words. Applause burst out and a score or more Confederate flags were raised and waved.

This intrusion of sound into the wheelhouse served to puncture the capsule which isolated Garner and the cavalry lieutenant from the rest of the world. And to the man's credit, the major made a fast decision and acted upon it with speed.

'Do as the Lieutenant says, Corporal!' he rasped, dropping his hand away from his holstered revolver and moving from the side to the front of the wheelhouse, snatching up the end of the speaking tube.

Dickson disappeared from sight, a look of glorious relief spreading across his acned face.

'Take the wheel, mister,' Garner ordered. 'And when I say hard over, I mean hard over.' He uncapped the tube, whistled down it and did not wait for acknowledgement before demanding: 'Up anchor and slow ahead, Mr Crennell.'

The winch clanked and the anchor chain rattled. The engines throbbed with a little more urgency, the sternwheel began to thrash at the water and the whole boat shuddered as man-made and river power struggled against each other – evenly matched.

'Hold her steady, Mr Steele,' Garner ordered without turning around, his eyes fixed upon that point in the river's bend where the Union vessels would first show.

Steele peered in the same direction, having to use every reserve of strength to turn the helm fractionally to left and right, as the current threatened to veer the foreshortened ram off line with the tall elm at which he had chosen to keep it aimed.

There was no opportunity now for memories, good or bad. Or for dwelling on personal animosities. For nervous tension kept a firm grip on the minds of every man aboard the *Pride of Memphis*. And either excited or terrified him as he waited and watched or listened.

Adam Steele was terrified. Not just frightened, as he had been on other occasions when he waited for the first shots of battle to be fired. For then he had been in an element he knew and understood. An experienced horseman astride a fine mount. Or on his own two feet with solid and predictable ground beneath them.

But this was different.

A riverboat with his gloved hands on the wheel. He would

93

be given orders by a man experienced in doing battle this way. And other orders would be given to the men in the engine room and those at the howitzers. But unless Steele responded as required and placed the *Pride of Memphis* in the position Garner demanded, the men below would be powerless.

'Full ahead!' Garner screamed down the speaking tube. 'Steady as she goes, Steele! Ready forward guns, Corporal!'

The orders only served to make the Virginian even more aware of the responsibility that was his. And then, for a fraction of a second – as the tempo of the engine noise and splashing of the sternwheel increased – he experienced a flash of understanding for Major Garner. An artillery officer who might well be good at his job in command of a conventional battery on dry land. But out of his element and hating it aboard this clumsy and top-heavy ironclad, in which he had lost half his men and sustained serious damage in his first engagement with the enemy. And realising, as he listened to the constant barrage of gunfire at Fort Pillow, that his second engagement would inevitably be a suicide mission.

Had he been a better officer he would not have sought release of his frustrations by humiliating his inferiors. But he was a good enough one to carry out his orders.

'Fire at will, Corporal!'

'Fire at will!' Dickson relayed.

And the two forward placed howitzers exploded shells out over the prow of the ironclad.

'Ready for a hard over to the left, Mr Steele.'

Garner was in total control of himself now. He shouted just loudly enough for Dickson to hear the orders to be relayed to the gun deck. And spoke close to conversational level to Steele.

'Yes, sir,' the Virginian acknowledged tautly, as the elm tree he had used to align the boat's course was suddenly obscured by a great spout of water and then a cloud of smoke. And his mind and body were freed of what he thought had been a paralysing fear – as the crash of the howitzers' firing faded to be replaced by a great cheer from the bank.

'Damn crazy civilians!' Garner snarled softly. 'Don't they know they could get their asses shot off!'

Then Steele saw the Union boats for the first time. Like the *Pride of Memphis* they were civilian craft converted for military use. One a sternwheeler and the other driven by an inboard wheel amidships. It was the latter which had been damaged by a howitzer shell, but although black smoke continued to billow from the jagged hole in her forward deck she maintained the same speed as the other boat. Both of them on a steady parallel curved course as they steamed out of the bend and on to the straight stretch of river where the Rebel craft had been anchored for so long.

Then, as a deafening barrage of artillery fire filled the late afternoon air, the Union boats sheered away from each other. The sternwheeler swinging wide out into midstream, while the other one surged along a collision course with *Pride of Memphis*.

'I knew it, I frigging knew it!' Garner yelled, his spirits rising to the high level of excitement which Dickson had enjoyed in anticipating the battle. 'The stupid bastards are doing just what I expected!'

He shot a glance over his shoulder, as Union shells erupted spouts of water ahead and to the port side of the boat. And Steele saw the broad grin on the florid face of a man who was like a stranger to the Garner he had known before.

'Prepare to change course, mister!' he bellowed above the crash of his own guns. 'Brace yourself to take hits!'

Garner himself hooked his hands over the lower rim of the slit and set his feet wide apart. While Steele splayed his own legs and took a tighter grip on the wheel spokes – as he saw spurts of smoke from the forward facing gunports of the boat directly ahead.

'Ready the starboard guns!' Garner shrieked.

'Ready to starboard!' Dickson relayed.

'Hard over left, mister!'

Steele spun the wheel, heard the crash of fired Union guns and felt the impact of shells smashing against the iron plating of the *Pride of Memphis*.

'Fire starboard, Dickson! Midships, Mr Steele!'

'Fire, men!' the corporal shrieked. 'Give the bastards hell, boys!'

The Confederate ironclad had come about in a ninety degree turn at full ahead speed, so that as Steele spun the wheel too far and struggled to correct the course, he saw beyond the head and shoulders of Garner and realised that it was the Union sternwheeler that was in their path, sideways on to them.

'Fire forward!'

'Fire forward!' Dickson echoed.

'Brace for ramming, men!' Garner yelled, and as the corporal repeated his words, the major shouted them again into the speaking tube.

Steele, his weariness, pain and discontent totally forgotten, experienced the same sense of exhilarated excitement he could hear in the voices of Garner and Dickson as he saw how well the plan was working.

A well-conceived plan put into operation with clockwork precision which had taken account of the probable tactics of the Union boats: that the officers aboard them had seen smoke above the trees, assumed the presence of an enemy vessel and decided upon a two-pronged attack. But the smoke which had been spotted had given no indication of the state of readiness of the *Pride of Memphis*. And the speed with which the Rebel ironclad had opened the engagement, followed by the abrupt change of course, had allowed the Union gunners to find the range for just one salvo.

But it was a tactical stand doomed to result in the destruction of the *Pride of Memphis* and perhaps the death of every member of her crew. Every man aboard surely had to be as aware of this fate as Steele and Garner, but it did not show in their actions as the river battle neared its climax.

For every gun on the starboard side and the two placed forward continued to blast shells out of the ports as fast as it was possible for spent cases to be ejected and fresh rounds loaded. While Crennell's engine room crew delivered maximum power to the thrashing sternwheel. And the two officers in the wheelhouse maintained a relentless course aimed at ramming the Union sternwheeler amidships.

And only now, as the watery gap between the prow of the *Pride of Memphis* and the port side of the enemy sternwheeler narrowed to twenty yards, did the men aboard the Union vessels realise that the Rebel plan had been conceived with the full knowledge that it would almost inevitably result in self-destruction. For only lucky direct hits on the sternwheel of one Union boat and into the engine room of the other could possibly have saved the *Pride of Memphis*.

But Garner had not counted on luck and he did not get it. What he and his crew and their vessel did get was a punishing bombardment of Union shells from dead ahead and off the starboard beam.

The din was like nothing else Steele had ever heard, even at Rich Mountain or Shiloh – at the moment of collision realising he was now at the centre of the kind of ghastly waking nightmare which he had been aware of at a distance for a large part of the day.

The sounds of the ram and the prow of the *Pride of Memphis* hitting the side of the Union sternwheeler before splitting her bulkheads and sinking deep into her, was almost in pleasant contrast to the constant crash and smash of exploded and exploding shells.

And Steele grinned. A fleeting expression of the enormous sense of satisfaction he derived from seeing the terror on the face of a Union gunner just before he was crushed under the weight of a toppling artillery piece.

Then the Virginian was gripped by the fear of death himself, as the *Pride of Memphis* was brought to an abrupt halt by the collision. And shuddered like a living thing from stem to stern – to send every man sprawling to the deck, flinging him forward to crash against anything immovable in his path.

Those men that had been on their feet. The majority were not. At the moment of ramming had already done with suffering. Lay sprawled, whole or with limbs, head and mutilated pieces of their bodies spread about them on the gun deck. Unaware of the pools and rivulets of blood which moved with the motion of the boat. Not seeing the holes which enemy shells had pierced in the plating, to open up great expanses of the early evening sky and wide views of the broad Mississippi, the tree-lined banks and the two Union ironclads – one ahead and the other alongside their doomed vessel: port guns blasting more death and destruction, until the new sounds of the collision curtailed the barrage.

All but one of the Rebel howitzers had been silenced by then, the rest of the guns in mangled ruins or their crews dead. Then, as Cross and Morris prepared to fire a final shot, they were hurled away from their gun by the collision and a Union shell whistled cleanly through a jagged hole and smashed into the boiler. And a powerful spray of scalding water seared the skin off their flesh before the blast flung their corpses against a bulkhead with bone-shattering force.

Corporal Dickson witnessed this double death from where

he lay on the deck, clinging on to the lowest rung of the ladder beneath the wheelhouse. And screamed his horror before he shrieked, 'Major!'

The single word issued from his gaping mouth in the same tone a dying man might use to call for his mother or wife.

But if Garner heard the plea, he gave no sign of it, as he struggled to sit up in one corner of the wheelhouse where he had been hurled by the collision. And grinned across at Steele who was on his hands and knees in another corner.

'A fine job, mister,' the senior officer yelled above the teeth-gritting sounds of metal against metal, the roar of flames from a fire in the engine room, the screams of wounded men, the thrashing of wheel paddles through water and the excited cheers of civilians on the bank. 'We can die knowing we did our duty, wouldn't you say?'

'Better to live and keep on doing it, sir,' the Virginian rasped, as he staggered to his feet and managed to reach the starboard side slit in the wheelhouse plating, before his strength gave out and he started to fall – hauled himself erect with his hands hooked over the bottom edge of the opening.

The Union ironclad with her paddle wheel amidships was no longer directly off the starboard beam. Instead was steaming fast across the stern of the craft into which the *Pride of Memphis* was locked: her guns silent and many of her crew out on deck with lines in their hands.

'What's happening, mister?' Garner demanded, trying to claw himself upright against the plating but hampered by a left arm that hung limp and broken at his side.

'They're set on picking up survivors, Major,' the Virginian answered. 'Let's get off before she sinks.'

'No, mister!' Garner snapped back, and his round, florid face became deep-set with a scowl. 'Get below to the gun deck! We haven't finished yet!'

The shell-holed ironclad still had smoke pouring from

her forward deck, but her engine continued to turn her wheel and she responded to the helm – coming about and sliding from Steele's sight beyond the crippled sternwheeler.

The Virginian staggered to the hatchway, saving his argument as he started down and then paused to see if Garner needed help.

'Move your ass, mister!' the major snarled as his scowl became a grimace of pain.

Feeling the old animosity toward the man, Steele continued to hold his tongue as he went down the ladder and viewed the scene of twisted metal and mangled bodies below with cold eyes.

'We're all that's left, sir,' Dickson groaned, with tears coursing across cheeks which were waxen and chalky white among the angry red blotches of his acne. 'Everyone down in the engine room just has to be dead.'

Garner fell heavily down the last few rungs of the ladder, remained upright by grabbing at Steele's shoulder with his good hand. Ordered: 'Each man to a port gun! Wait for my command.'

Flames roared, steam hissed and metal creaked as the locked-together ironclads settled lower in the water. This against a clamour of shouting voices and a rumble of engines held in check as the surviving Union boat took aboard men from the doomed vessel. Hearing all this, and aware for the first time of the smell of steam and smoke and blood, Steele strained his ears to catch screams of pain or calls for help aboard the *Pride of Memphis*. There were none and he rasped at Garner:

'You said a fine job, sir! There's nothing we can do to better it now!'

'Nonsense, mister! We have guns on the port side which did not fire a shot in this engagement! As soon as the second Union boat is in their sights, we'll blow her out of the water!'

100

He released his hold on Steele's shoulder and lurched across the gun deck, zigzagging between the sprawled corpses and dismembered limbs. Dickson made to follow him, but froze when the Virginian snarled:

'We're locked into the other boat, Major! Drifting! Without power! We can't bring the guns to bear unless they steam into the sights! Soon as we fire a shot they can turn and throw everything they have at us!'

Dickson turned his youthful face from Steele to Garner, to Steele, and then fixed his stare on the suddenly enraged face of the major.

'You're a coward, mister!' Garner yelled across the ravaged gun deck as he reached out and leaned against a howitzer. 'I've said it from the damn start! You abandoned your own men to their slaughter and escaped to save your own rotten skin! You will not desert under fire this time, you damn sonofabitch! I'll see to that! Phil, man a gun!'

Corporal Dickson continued to remain rooted to the spot like some lifelike replica of a frightened young man. Squeezed his eyes tightly closed and then snapped them open again and gasped – at the sight of Garner with a Colt revolver in his hand: aimed at Steele.

The sound of a rumbling engine changed note, and paddles thrashed at water as the surviving Union ironclad started downriver again.

'Die like the craven coward you are, you snotnose sonofabitch!' Garner raged.

And squeezed the trigger.

The bullet from the bucking revolver would probably not have missed the Virginian had he remained where he was. But he hurled himself to the deck in reflex action, cursing as he heard the lead richocet twice against metal.

Garner's curse was louder and shriller as he thumbed back the hammer for a second shot.

The Derringer was trapped in Steele's pocket. Death

stared him in the face again, but a part of his mind remained clear enough to receive the impulse that told him the length of the knife was pressing against his leg.

'No, sir!' Dickson yelled. 'The Lieutenant's right! We can't win.' He stepped into the line of fire. 'There'll be other blue-bellies in other places, sir!'

'Move aside or I'll kill you too, Phil!' Garner snarled.

Steele reached down and clawed at the cuff of his pants leg. Heard the seam stitching rent and fisted a gloved hand around the knife handle.

'Sir!' Dickson screamed.

The Colt exploded again and Dickson hurled himself to the decking. To give Steele a clear view of the enraged major, the howitzer and, beyond the barrel of the gun, the stern of the Union ironclad with the white water of her wake streaming out behind.

On the bank, the watching southern sympathisers booed and hissed and whistled. But these sounds were masked after a moment by a rush of water: as the locked vessels settled low enough in the river for torrents to pour into them from many quarters.

Garner cocked his Colt again.

Steele hurled the knife. Inexpertly and with no hope of inflicting a wound on the target. But the action caused Garner to duck and turn to evade the missile. His gun hand cracked against the howitzer breach and the revolver flew clear of the jarred knuckles. Instead of pain, though, it was the anger of frustration that powered the sound coming from his throat – as he glimpsed the Union boat making away at full speed.

'You sonsofbitches stay and fight!' he screamed. And fired the shell already loaded into the howitzer's breech.

The trajectory of the shot was high and wide, causing a water spout thirty yards ahead and twenty yards to the left of the ironclad's bow.

'Help me reload, help me reload you bastards!' Garner implored as he used his good hand to open the breach and eject the shellcase in a billow of acrid powder smoke. But knew he had no chance of lifting and fitting a fresh twelve pounder.

The Union boat did not change course or reduce speed and it was obvious the men at her aft guns had been maintaining a careful watch on the *Pride of Memphis*, constantly changing the rake of their barrels.

Twin puffs of smoke spurted at the gun ports.

Garner, a stream of obscenities coming from his trembling lips, continued to struggle with a shell.

Steele and Dickson both lunged to their feet and raced for the starboard side of the boat. The lieutenant to one gun port and the corporal to another.

Both shots scored simultaneous hits against the port side of the Rebel boat. One opened up a fresh hole in her hull so that more water could gush in and hasten her sinking. The other pierced the gun deck bulkhead and cut Major Garner in two at the waist, as he turned to try to sprint in the wake of Steele and Dickson.

These men were unaware of exactly how he met his end. They just knew that he was certainly dead, and at that moment, the latest of many since the battle began, they briefly considered their own ends before blast from the exploding shells lifted them bodily off the gunwale of the *Pride of Memphis* and flung them far out across the river.

They felt the rush of air around them, heard the crash and saw trees and water and sky in a confused blur as they twisted and turned. Next were aware of the vicious slap of their helpless bodies slamming into the surface of the river. Hard enough to end awareness of anything else.

Just as in the tiny cabin aboard the ironclad, Steele felt he had been withdrawn from the waking world for a few seconds when a man said 'You're all right, son. You're going to be just fine.'

He opened his eyes and the pitch darkness was relieved just a little: enough for him to see the face of a man with grey sidewhiskers and a strained, anxious smile on his face. Looking down at him from a few inches away. All around there were other people. Towering figures with their heads and shoulders silhouetted against the night sky.

'You hear what I'm saying, son?' the man asked. 'Everything is just fine. You're all right.'

'I'm glad about that,' Steele answered huskily and tried to spread a smile across his own face. Sensed it was lopsided as he added, 'For awhile there I had this real bad sinking feeling.'

CHAPTER SIX

'WE could've sunk both them damn bluebelly boats if it wasn't for him! The Major was gonna do it! Would've, too! If that bastard hadn't've killed him before he had the chance!'

There was a scuffle among the group surrounding Steele. And a babble of voices, some placating and some angry, as the Virginian struggled up into a sitting posture: had to accept the offered support of the man with the sidewhiskers to keep from falling down on to his back again.

'Grateful to you, feller,' he said, and dragged himself up on to his feet, still using more of the other man's strength than his own. Then received support from the other side and the back as he swayed and his legs began to buckle. And for long moments, Dickson's accusing voice was little more than a drone against a babble of protesting words which seemed to be trying to drown it out: while Steele struggled to beat the demands of his mind and body for rest.

'He's a traitor, I tell you . . . since he come aboard . . . some story about losin' all his men . . . Major Garner, he never did truly believe him . . . reckon he's a bluebelly really who . . . tried to fix it so both them . . . man like that oughta be strung up.'

Steele became aware of his sopping wet clothing and of

the coldness of his flesh. Of water seeping out of his hair and trickling down his face. Of physical pain that was more insistent than mental exhaustion. Of the sounds of the gently flowing river which were all that now competed with the angrily shrill tones of the young non-com's words. And of the tense silence that gripped the large gathering of people which encircled Dickson and himself.

For several more stretched seconds the Virginian continued to keep his eyes tightly closed as he struggled to will strength into his punished body. And during this time he began to comprehend every word the corporal said – instead of merely disjointed snatches of the young man's diatribe.

'Corporal!' he rasped at length, as he snapped open his eyes. And saw Dickson glaring angrily at him across twenty feet of trampled grass. Looked about him and saw a mixture of expressions on the faces of men, women and children who had backed away from him since he had risen to his feet. And who retreated still further, those at the front pressing those behind, now that he had regained some degree of self-control. There was fear and pity on the faces, curiosity and anguish, suspicion and anger. He looked beyond the encircling crowd and saw in the murky twilight of the spring evening the trees and the river – the latter placid now that the battle was long over: with just a piece of drifting timber here and there to show that two riverboats had sunk helplessly below the surface. Perhaps not all the flotsam out there was timber – maybe upon closer examination might be seen to be parts of the men who had died with the vessels. But Steele had neither the time nor the inclination to look that closely. 'The Major's dead, Corporal. So, too is Lieutenant Crennell. You are now under my command.'

The man behind Steele and to his right released their holds on him and backed off.

'You all right now, son?' the man with sidewhiskers asked.

'Reckon I can stand, sir,' the Virginian answered. And was allowed to test the claim, although his prime helper remained at his side.

'We ain't in the army, mister!' a beefily-built, red-faced man close to Dickson snarled. 'So we don't have to take no orders from you! And after seein' you jump off that boat like a scared chicken while her guns were still firin', I figure you oughta give an account of yourself!'

There were nods and vocal murmurs of agreement. More of them and more insistent than the competing signs and sounds of support for Steele. Until the well-dressed man beside the Virginian silenced the crowd with a snarled:

'Shut up, the whole lot of you!' And then glowered around to consolidate his position as the centre of attention. Cleared his throat and moderated his tone to continue, 'There's not one of us here except for the Lieutenant and the Corporal who knows what happened out on the river awhile back. Except that the CSA boat perished while sinking a Union craft. She was doomed from the start, but she went down fighting impossible odds and she inflicted harsh punishment on the enemy. To little avail to my mind. Since the action cost many lives and, in broad military terms, was no more than a floating tree trunk in the path of the inevitable advance of the Yankees down the Mississippi.'

Some of his audience began to shuffle their feet, while others gave rasping voice to the expressions of impatience on their faces as the man with sidewhiskers began to sound like a lecturer warming to a favourite subject. Steele's initial gratitude became undermined by a brand of resentment that his position was being used as a platform.

'All right, all right!' the speaker went on, waving his big hands to still the disquiet. 'This is neither the time nor the place. But many of you know of my military experience. So believe me when I say that soldiers of other ranks quite often have no love for their officers. And I think we should be on our way and allow these gallant soldiers to rejoin others of their kind and continue the struggle against the oppressors of the Northern states. And I say again that . . . '

'He'll kill me if you do!' Dickson blurted out. 'He's a Yankee spy, I tell you. He killed my . . . the Major. And because I saw him do that he'll kill me, too. If he gets the chance.'

There was another clamorous chorus of support for Dickson and Steele felt as if he was swaying with the waves of sound that buffetted him. But he ignored the large body of civilians, whose sense of triumph at the sinking of the Union ironclad was counterbalanced by the bitterness of seeing the *Pride of Memphis* go down, too. Instead, concentrated his level gaze on the acned face of Dickson: recalling how the corporal had maybe saved his life by stepping into the line of fire from Garner's Colt. But that had not been the young soldier's prime motive, of course. Rather, he had been intent upon urging Garner to abandon ship: and to do so without first committing an act of murder he would later regret. Knowing the major even better than Steele did: aware of the two diametrically opposed sides of the man's character.

But Dickson had failed to save the life of the man who had been much more to him than a commanding officer. Obscenely more than that. And had himself survived. Filled with grief and remorse which needed an outlet more powerful than the shedding of tears. Seeing Steele, who had caused him to leave Garner to his violent fate, as a means of release.

'Don't give him the chance!' a man yelled from the rear of the crowd to Steele's right. 'There's plenty of trees around here! String up the sonofabitch!'

'No!'

'That's disgusting!'

'I'm leaving! Come on, bring the children!'

'Yeah, lynch the spy!'

'Come off that boat like a rat while the guns was still blastin'!'

Against the barrage of voices – angry and afraid, protesting and gleeful – Adam Steele fastened his mind upon that of the man who had triggered the revival of the conflict. And sought to hear it again in the clamour, as his eyes raked over the faces in an effort to spot the man. A man he was certain he knew.

But the past from which the partial memory sprang was too clouded by violent events and the present was too menacing to allow time and opportunity for concentrating on side issues. Because the crowd were closing in around him.

Not the women and children. Nor the majority of the men, he saw, as he swung his eyes to left and right and then shot a look over his shoulder. But enough. Twenty or so men with ugly scowls on their faces. Middle-aged and elderly men. Like all those who had gathered in the clearing to watch the battle on the river.

The younger element from the locality would all be in uniform, he guessed. And felt anger at allowing such a superfluous consideration to occupy his mind.

Dickson held back, and was suddenly isolated in an area left clear by that part of the crowd which moved towards Steele and that which backed away. There was no sign of triumph on his spot-ravaged face. Just grief and anguish. But his no longer bright eyes offered nothing when they met and briefly held the level gaze of Steele.

Then the Virginian saw a familiar face and matched it to the voice which had triggered the move to tighten the circle around him. Jim Haven, who had been so disgruntled with his wagon-guarding chore as he smoked a cheroot outside the hotel in Attrill.

Steele caught a brief glimpse of the man in the widening outer circle of civilians, before he was obscured by men and women anxious to detach themselves from the impending violence by putting space between it and themselves.

Then clawed hands reached out for the Virginian and he tried to step back. But found escape blocked by a wall of solid bodies. A moment later was gripped from behind, as those in front and to either side of him clasped his arms, shoulders and his sodden uniform tunic.

He felt hot breath on his face as rasped obscenities beat against his eardrums. He made to struggle, but then felt paralysed by terror when a man behind him said grimly:

'We ain't got a friggin' rope.'

He squeezed his eyes tightly closed, aware of the humiliating tears that he was trapping behind the lids: knowing that his weeping would be misconstrued by the men bent on killing him and by the watchers.

For they were sure to view such tears as those of a coward. Could not be expected in the circumstances to realise that Adam Steele's self-pity was less concerned with the act of dying than with the manner of the act. That he was enduring the anguish of having survived the carnage of enemy action only to meet an undeserved end at the hands of those who shared his cause and aims. In the knowledge that to defend himself with the truth – shouting of the perverted relationship between Dickson and Garner that was behind the corporal's lying accusations – would only serve to inflame the passions of the naïve country people around him.

'Stand back, you crazy men! If you don't stand back, God knows how many of you will die!'

This voice was easier to place and Steele knew who had spoken the words before the gunshot cracked out. The man with the grey sidewhiskers who had come to his aid at the outset.

Several hands released him as the demand was shouted. The rest when the shot exploded.

Steele opened his eyes and felt the moisture in them as

he swung his head: looked between two of his would-be lynchers and saw the man in the act of bringing the revolver to level it at the group.

'You talk up a storm for the South, Byers!' a man close to Steele snarled. 'But when it comes to the . . .'

'Hold your tongue, sir!' Byers cut in, the flesh of his face trembling but his hand holding the revolver rock still. 'Whatever the merits or otherwise of the Corporal's case, it is not up to any of us to judge it. This is a military matter to be dealt with by the military. I beseech you to hand over both these men to their superiors – if you must take any action at all. If you do not, then I will . . .'

'You won't do nothin', Byers! If you start shootin', you'll likely hit this Yankee . . .'

'Go to it, men! String him up! He's a spy for Lincoln and the rest of them Union sonsofbitches!'

It was Haven again, inciting murder as he shoved his way clear of the press of people and advanced into the clearing that was now lit softly by the rising half moon: vengeance gleaming in his eyes, as he looked through a gap and locked his stare on the pale, haggard face of the Virginian.

'Stranger's right, Clyde!' a man close to Steele snarled. 'We gotta do it! For the South! If Byers starts shootin', them of us that are left will take care of the bastard!'

Clawed hands reached for and took tight grips on Steele again. And determined voices roared approval of what had been said.

Then another voice which rang a chord in the Virginian's memory yelled shrilly:

'Now girl! Aim it girl! Tell me when! I'll do it!'

If the girl said anything, it was not heard by anyone except the man who made the demands on her. Then a gunshot exploded to prelude a hard silence that seemed to last for an eternity. Not from the pistol in the iron grip of Byers. Not a pistol at all. Much louder and lower in tone. To blast buckshot from the muzzle of a shotgun.

Hands let go of Steele and the men scrambled away from him: perhaps fearful that the gun had sprayed its lethal charge toward their group. But it was Jimmy Haven who was sent sprawling to the ground, his corpse erupting blood from countless wounds in the right side of his face and arm and torso. The man from Attrill falling away from the two people who stood so close together they looked like one in the moon-shadowed clearing.

'He's dead, grandpa,' the girl said dully, to break the tense silence, as she took her hands off the shotgun with the still-smoking muzzle and stepped away from the back of the Attrill ferryman.

And the old man nodded and swung his head to left and right: staring sightlessly and unafraid at the many people whom he knew were watching him.

'The man I just killed and a whole lot of others and their women folk ambushed and murdered a troop of Confederate soldiers last night,' he said, and his words silenced the start of shocked vocal reaction to the new killing. 'Soldiers that were takin' much needed supplies upriver. Ammunition for Confederate guns. That feller you people are so set on hangin', he had the good fortune not to be murdered by Attrill folks. And he got into town where the wagons were took and he blew them into a million pieces. To make sure the Yankees didn't lay hands on all that ammunition. Made thirty kids motherless and killed three kids in the process. But then it ain't always the guilty that suffer in times of war.'

Steele's body and mind had gradually started to tingle with rising hope as he listened to the old ferryman's words and saw the expressions of horror which spread across many faces of the watchers. Then he yet again had to make a physical effort to quell the threat of nausea when his suspicion about certain victims of the explosion at Attrill was confirmed. And he heard the final words of the blind man as if they reached his ears from down a long tunnel.

'I done my killin' and I said my piece. Now me and my granddaughter aim to leave if we're allowed. Not to go back to Attrill, where we've been accused of helpin' the Lieutenant and sent packin'. Up to you if you let us go. Up to you if you believe me. Up to you whether you go to Attrill and find out what happened. I done my best and so did the girl here.'

'Thank you, sir!' Byers called huskily. 'I pray to God it will be enough to keep these people from doing something that will haunt them for the rest of . . .'

'Where's the other one?'

'Yeah, the Corporal?'

'Speak up, youngster.'

'He must have some reason to . . .'

'He ain't here no more!'

From close to Steele and from the fringe of the clearing the voices were raised, the words spoken with mounting anger as the men who asked the questions and made the demands searched for and failed to locate Corporal Dickson. Until suddenly there was another silence, disturbed only by the gurgling of the river and the slow footfalls of the ferryman and his granddaughter moving away through the timber.

Then the men close to the Virginian backed away from him, shoulders sagging and eyes averted.

'The man has run!' Byers pronounced, thrusting his revolver into a pocket of his long frock coat. 'Could there not be more clear evidence of his perfidy? And now those of you who were about to consign a true Southern patriot to such an ignominious end should also run. To your homes where you should reflect upon the grievous crime you almost committed. And then give your thanks to God for . . .'

'All right, Mr Byers,' the man who had been the ringleader of those who moved against Steele cut in grimly.

'Maybe we ain't able to put words to our thoughts like you are. But we can do our own thinkin'.' He paused in moving away from the Virginian and managed to look him in the eye to offer: 'I'm sorry, mister. We're all sorry. But it looked real bad for you.'

The young lieutenant's face was still set in the expression created by the certain knowledge that he had blasted three children to death in his first independent action against a wartime enemy. And his feelings of self-revulsion seemed to be directed at his erstwhile would-be lynchers when he growled:

'It didn't look so damn good from where I was watching, feller.'

CHAPTER SEVEN

THERE were countless offers of unspecified help after Steele staggered to the stump of a recently felled tree and lowered himself wearily and painfully on to it. Which he refused with shakes of his buzzing head or curt negative sounds and words. Occasionally, his blunt reception of attempts to make amends drew snarling counterreactions from men and women who compared their own circumstances with his. So that as he rested, easing his aching muscles and struggling to come to terms with what he had done and what had been done to him, he heard disjointed and half-completed tales of other people's woes. From which it emerged that just a handful of the civilians lived locally and that most were refugees from further north, fleeing before the Union forces which were sweeping into and across Tennessee.

They had gathered on the bank of the Mississippi to watch the battle of the ironclads not out of mere morbid curiosity: but in hope of seeing the Yankees beaten or driven back – to witness a Confederate victory from which they might draw hope for the future after hearing nothing but bad news for so long.

While he rested on the tree stump as evening gave way to full night and the crowd dispersed, Steele was not consciously aware that he was assimilating any details of what was being said to him. He could not even be certain that he did not doze fitfully as he sat in a dejected attitude, back arched, elbows on his knees and bristled chin cupped in his gloved hands. Certainly, though, he was not aware that he and the bewhiskered Byers were alone in the clearing with the shattered corpse of Jimmy Haven until his attention was called to the fact.

'Well, son, you turned down a lot of well meaning people,' the man said with a sigh. 'And all I've got to offer you is advice. Which is to report back to your commanding officer or run the risk of ending up like that unfortunate gentleman.'

The Virginian raised his head and shook it to try to rid himself of the disconcerting buzzing tone in his ears. He couldn't and he looked from Byers to the river, the clearing as a whole, to the dark hump that was the blasted body of the man from Attrill.

'Not that you might not die violently among your comrades on some far off battlefield, Lieutenant,' the man in the frock coat allowed. 'But better that than to be murdered in some lonely place by person or persons with reason to detest the uniform you wear.'

Steele nodded and rose tentatively to his feet, testing each muscle before depending upon it to play its full part in keeping him upright.

'Grateful to you, feller,' he said as he once more became uncomfortably aware of the wet clothing pressing coldly against his flesh. 'For everything.'

Byers sighed and his face expressed deep regret. 'I've done little enough, Lieutenant Steele. Spent a useful lifetime in the army but was retired when my time came. Three years ago last Monday. Too old to be taken back, a mere Captain, for active service at the outset of the South's struggle for independence. But I do what I am able – journeying through the Confederate states and lecturing on how everyone, man, woman and child, may aid the Cause.' He sighed again, but now he showed a smile of pride. 'And perhaps this evening I reached my greatest achievement. By actually assisting in saving the life of one of our fighting men.'

Steele abruptly felt young and inadequate as well as weary and weak as the seasoned ex-soldier beamed at him. 'I'll try to do better next time, sir,' he promised.

'Better, Lieutenant?' Byers asked, perplexed.

'Corporal Dickson could have been right. I did disobey the order of a superior officer. And retreated under fire to leave the Major to fight the enemy single . . . '

'Lieutenant Steele!' Byers snapped, in such a tone of authority that the Virginian came to attention in a reflex action. And in the moonlight-alleviated darkness thought he detected a brief smile cross the old soldier's face: certainly heard Byers continue to address him in the manner of a superior officer talking down to his junior. 'I know what I saw from the point of view of a bystander. Which was a splendidly successful effort by an outnumbered force to harry the enemy. What happened aboard your craft after the ramming incident I do not know and do not wish to know. What I saw from my viewpoint was an humane action by one of the enemy craft in picking up survivors before withdrawing. And that is what you did, Lieutenant – you withdrew. You did not retreat. Withdrew so that you survived to fight another day. One man – you say your commanding officer – remained aboard. And I saw him attempt an impossible mission, that doomed himself and whoever else remained aboard to inevitable death.'

Steele was no longer at rigid attention, but he stayed on the same spot, swinging his head from left to right as Byers paced to and fro in front of him.

'To disobey an order, especially during action, is an unpardonable sin, son,' the man went on. 'Many high command

117

officers who have never seen a shot fired in anger are inclined to think that this applies in every circumstance. But such men are narrow-minded fools. This afternoon's engagement was no last-ditch attempt to keep the enemy from winning the war or even a strategically important battle. It was a minor incident of absolutely no consequence . . . except to those men who died and their loved ones who will grieve for them.

'My God, the Union craft that was gone downriver did not carry an entire army. And the sinking of two other craft at this point will not block the channel to prevent the Union's entire Western Flotilla from coming through whenever it is ordered to do so!

'No, Lieutenant!' Byers continued angrily. 'Have no regrets or self-doubts about today. You took part in a minor engagement, bravely fought on both sides. With inevitable casualties. And the commander of the Union ironclad acted admirably in rescuing his comrades and disengaging from the battle when he considered it pointless to continue. Just as you are to be commended for electing to withdraw when you did: setting an example which the young Corporal followed.'

'I'll try to think of it that way, sir,' Steele allowed.

'Do that, son,' Byers murmured and suddenly looked and sounded as weary as the younger man felt. 'But I'm afraid you'll have no other opportunities to act the way you did today. Should you ever have the misfortune to serve under another gallant and crazy sonofabitch like this Major Garner. And there are many of them in your army, Mr Steele. Death or glory officers who see their men as no more than extensions of the weapons in the men's hands. All you can do, son, is try to steer clear of that kind. And at all costs, don't become one of them. Remember the Alamo, by all means. But remember it only in terms of what might have happened if those fine, brave men had lived to fight on a better day. Here, take this.'

118

He had shrugged out of his frock coat as he reached the conclusion of his part military, part paternal monologue. And now he thrust it toward the Virginian.

'A little on the large size, I guess. But it'll serve as a blanket while you sleep and your uniform dries. And hide the uniform until you reach somewhere you can be seen for what you are without being in danger. I'd head for Corinth, if I were you, son. Way I see it, with Fort Pillow done for, the Union will push hard downriver to Memphis. And they can make good time on water. A general named Halleck is in command of their land forces and he's a slow mover by all accounts. Doesn't cross his bridges until he reaches them, and won't even admit there's a bridge there until ten scouts have confirmed it. Reports are that Beauregard's still at Corinth after the Shiloh fiasco. But he's got less than half Halleck's strength and is likely to pull out before the Yankees get there. A wiser officer than your Major Garner, uh?'

Byers grinned as he touched briefly on the subject that had occupied him earlier. Then raised a hand and swung around to head out of the clearing.

'You're going back north, sir?' Steele called after him, the older man's coat still draped over an arm.

'The Confederacy has got plenty of men to the south, son!' Byers answered without looking back. 'No need of me in that direction.'

Then he was gone, lost among the shadows under the trees. And soon the sound of his footfalls was out of earshot.

For a long moment the Virginian continued to gaze at the point on the fringe of the clearing where Byers had disappeared from sight. Then he threw up a weary and unseen salute, draped the long coat over his shoulders and felt a weighty object in one of the packets. He took out the Colt Navy Model revolver which had played a part in saving his neck from the lynch rope and wondered for a while if the bewhiskered man had intended the gun to be a gift in the same way as the coat. Decided it had been, because Byers was the kind of man who would never do anything absent-mindedly. So he slid the Colt into his empty holster and set off to follow that part of the man's advice concerning Corinth being a better destination than Memphis.

He made just one deviation – at the outset – to see if the gelding he had hitched to a tree much earlier in the day was still there. He did not expect to find the animal and so he was not disappointed. Either the horse had wrenched free of its tether and bolted when the river battle was raging: or had been stolen by one of the refugees. Or maybe even Corporal Dickson.

Steele experienced no ill-feeling about the possibility of theft, for in truth that was how he had come to obtain the gelding. But the fact that the blind old ferryman bore him no ill-will over this had nothing to do with his own feelings now. It was simply that, in time of war, a man was entitled to do what he had to do in order to survive. And once he had learned this lesson from bitter experience, he could not frown upon others who had attended the same class. Friend or enemy.

He did not travel far that night. No more than two miles in a south-eastern direction. Every step he took required a disproportionate amount of energy, but he took it in the sure knowledge that the further he went from the river and the scene of the battle, the safer would be the place where he bedded down.

For other Attrill men might come after Haven. Other Union ironclads might steam around the bend in the river and pause to investigate the reason for the floating wreckage. Or forward patrols of the Union land force. Confederate deserters or fleeing civilians who were likely to value a sleeping soldier's meagre possessions more than his life.

Where he chose to sleep was under some brush beside a dirt road scored with old wheel ruts. And it was a good place because he slept soundly and undisturbed for a very long time. Came awake with a cry of alarm and opened his eyes to blinding light: thought for sweating seconds that the nightmare which had roused him was a continuing reality – that the light was from the flash of the explosion which tore apart the big house on the Steele plantation and obliterated every trace that his father, Diana Summers, Elroy, the other Negroes and their women had ever lived.

But it was only the rays of the midmorning sun, blazing down upon him through the lacework of foliage under which he had slept.

He listened. To birdcalls and the scurrying sounds of small woodland creatures going about their business of survival.

He tried to move and found he could not. Sweated more profusely as he lay sprawled on his back – recalling the events which had brought him to this place and seeking to fasten on some aspect of his suffering which could have left him paralysed. Knew there had been none, and with this knowledge firm in his mind made a fresh attempt to stir. And this time was able to roll over on to his belly and crawl out of his resting place: gritting his teeth against the painful protests made by an aching body that resented such demands after a long period of sublime inertia.

He got to his feet and shaded his eyes from the ten o'clock sun as he surveyed the rolling countryside of Western Tennessee which, apart from the rutted dirt road, showed no sign on this bright and warm spring morning that man had ever encroached upon it.

He felt – and guessed he looked – a great deal older than his twenty-five years. Physically, at least. But did not see an image of himself until after midday, when the dirt road he was following forded a shallow stream and he knelt down beside it – gazed bleakly at his reflection in the clear water for a moment before he cupped his hands to drink and to rinse his face.

His face was gaunt, the dirt-ingrained flesh puckered, the many hours of red and grey bristles long enough to appear the start of a beard. But it was in the eyes that he saw the greatest change which had come about. They seemed somehow more deep-set and like cold, dark stones incapable of expressing any emotion except that with which he examined his reflection – a brand of calculated callousness that he would previously have considered himself incapable of harbouring.

Then, after he had plunged his gloved hands into the stream, sucked up the cool water and thrown other handfuls into his face, he smiled. A smile which he was unable to see reflected in the disturbed surface of the stream, but which he felt in the tautness of his flesh as it drew his mouthline into a shape that matched the look he had seen in his eyes. For he abruptly realised that his mind had become as shaped by recent events as had his physical sensations and appearance.

And he splashed across the knee-deep stream and continued on along the dirt road with a buoyant feeling of being, if not in control, at least capable of facing up to his own destiny. For he was a fully fledged adult now and realised he had been deluding himself since he was twelve – when he had first decided he was grown up. And had been allowed by his indulgent father to continue to think of himself as such in the protected and privileged environment of the plantation.

But that had all been a charade. And his initial experiences of the war had been little more than an extension of the way he had lived on and around the Steele Plantation. Privileged to be a commissioned officer and taking full

122

advantage of his rights – in the sure and certain knowledge that there were countless substitute Ben Steeles, in the form of senior officers who made the important decisions and could countermand any of his that were inappropriate.

At Rich Mountain and at Shiloh.

But since he had been detailed to command the escort of the supply train he had been constantly aware of his own responsibilities and the total lack of higher authority to cover him. He had made mistakes. First in not knowing his men well enough to realise their potential to mutiny. Then in allowing himself to be seconded to Major Garner after deciding to ride for Fort Pillow. Next in waiting too long before making his move against Garner. Finally in allowing himself the luxury of self-pity during those moments when he felt sure he was on the verge of being lynched.

But each error had been rectified or countered, and as he headed south as fast as the need for caution allowed, he felt sure that on balance he was in credit. Realised he had needed Byers in the clearing last night to tell him so, while he endured the aftermath of terror that was manifest in remorse and depression and the total draining of self-assurance. Was not sure if such a booster to his morale would have been required on this bright day after a night's rest. But was entirely certain that he would never again need another substitute father figure.

Steele still had the military map of western Tennessee on which was marked the intended route of the supply train from Memphis to Pillow. It showed that section of the state between the Mississippi and Tennessee rivers and extended far enough south into Mississippi state to have Corinth marked – seen to be the best part of a hundred miles from where the Virginian had begun his trek. And he had to walk every one of those miles, for he elected to follow a diagonal route which kept him clear of towns along the Memphis and

Charleston Railroad to the south, and those which were strung out beside the Mobile and Ohio Railroad to the east. For although both tracks intersected at his destination he had no way of knowing if they were still operating, which side controlled them or the sympathies of the civilians in the towns.

So he walked, slept under brush or in dry ditches, drank water from clear streams and ate sparingly of a fat buck rabbit, which he brought down with a lucky shot from the Navy Colt late on that first afternoon.

And in the early evening of the fourth day, with old injuries healed, his strength replenished and his muscles toned by the exertion of the arduous trip, he came in sight of his objective. Looked down from a rise over which the tracks of the Mobile and Ohio Railroad skirted, saw the town of Corinth where he had arrived to take part in the battle of Shiloh – and retreated to after the fighting – and experienced a great surge of anger. An emotion so powerful that it demanded a vocal outlet in the form of a stream of obscenities. Heard only by his own ears on the deserted hill crest – far out of earshot of the men who were putting the town to the torch.

Not many men, but clear to see in the light of the leaping flames which licked against the advance of the night's dark. Men who moved with the frantic speed that suggested panic, as they sought to complete the task of burning down every building and bridge in Corinth.

Men in grey uniforms, carrying out orders and desperately anxious to have done with the detail: so that they could join the column of other uniformed men which was snaking southwards from the burning town. Heading down a road which ran parallel with the railroad along which a train was gathering speed – twin locomotives hauling a line of flatcars laden with artillery pieces.

How many men? How many guns? A great many. How

many trains and men had left ahead of these last to start south?

What did it matter?

Adam Steele stopped his cursing and brought his temper under control. Of course it mattered.

General Gustave Beauregard knew the strength of his command at Corinth and had decided to pull out from the town ahead of Halleck's advancing armies – taking care to burn anything that would be of use to the enemy. And without knowledge of the logistics of the situation which motivated Beauregard's decision, a mere lieutenant who had executed a less dramatic withdrawal a few days previously had to respect the general's point of view.

But it galled the Virginian to see such a massive body of Confederate troops turning their backs on the enemy without firing a shot. At least the crazy Major Garner had . . .

Steele jerked his mind back from this line of thought and had to make a conscious effort to alter his expression from what he knew to be a petulant set. He realised that he had started to think and look like an overgrown spoilt child again, reacting badly to a turn of events that went against his grain.

And he dropped down wearily on to his haunches and watched the burning of Corinth with impassive eyes – feeling a deep depression but not showing it. For perhaps fifteen minutes he remained there, as the flames spread and the smoke formed an ominous cloud above the town. Then, as the grey uniformed arsonists began to leave the scene of destruction and full night enclosed the area of bright burning, he rose and moved down the hill to the railroad: followed the tracks toward the northern fringe of town. And just before he stepped into the far reaches of the fire's glow he took off Byers' frock coat and placed his uniform cap on his head – realising there might well be sharpshooters positioned as rearguards for the departing army. Nervous soldiers with sweating palms and churning stomachs, knowing the Union army was near and resentful of the lonely and dangerous detail they had drawn – liable to trigger a shot at any human figure they saw unless it was instantly recognisable as one of their own kind.

But no shot was fired and no challenge rang out against the crackle of flames and the creaks and crashes of falling beams, as Steele entered the edge of town, with the stink of burning assaulting his nostrils and the heat of the surrounding fires drying the sweat of tension on his heavily-bristled face.

He was off the railroad tracks now, having veered to the left when he saw that one of the largest fires rose from the depot. And he had a firm objective in mind – a small frame church at the end of a side street. It was isolated from neighbouring buildings and had been ignored by the destroyers, perhaps on moral grounds or more likely because it would have no strategic value to the enemy.

Steele approached the single storey building with its short spire on the blind side to any watching sharpshooters: having to step over a low picket fence and then move between the grassy mounds of headstoned graves to reach the side of the church. He was exposed by the firelight again as he came around a front corner of the building and then was hidden in the shadowed porchway beneath the spire. The narrow double doors were latched, but swung easily open and then closed again behind him once he was inside.

He gave a low, whistling sigh of relief, closed his eyes for several seconds and then opened them to survey the interior of the church.

It was simply furnished and decorated for a congregation which worshipped in some branch of the Protestant faith. Dirt-floored with a narrow central aisle between a line of nine pews to either side. At the end of the aisle was an altar covered with a cloth on top of which stood two candlesticks.

To one side of the altar was a pulpit and to the other a small pump organ. Beyond it was an archway on to darkness, which held firm against the firelight that filtered through the plain glass windows in the side wall. All the furniture was painted black, while the walls and ceiling were whitened.

The church was cool and smelled clean. The sounds of the many raging fires were subdued and Adam Steele relished the peace and solitude of the place for several seconds before remembering to remove his cap. Then he advanced along the aisle, to carry out the purpose for which he had come here: having to force from his mind the insistent thought that the last time he had been in a church was to attend his mother's funeral, many years ago.

He walked between the altar and the organ and under the archway into the darkened area, taking one of the candles as he passed. He lit the wick and saw he was in a short and narrow passageway with a door to either side. Here the walls and ceiling were of unpainted timber.

One door opened on to a windowless room which contained a table piled with Bibles, hymnbooks, sheet music and a neat stack of hassocks in a corner. In the second he was able to extinguish the candle, since it had a window which admitted the light of the fires outside – firelight that caused his teeth to gleam between curled-back lips as he raked his impassive black eyes around the vestry.

There was a chair in front of a table which had been pushed back against a wall, with a mirror resting on the table. Also on the table was a basin and a pitcher half filled with water. And a pipe and almost exhausted pack of tobacco. From a hook in the wall nearby hung two complete sets of clerical vestments. And beyond this a shelf with two Bibles, two hymnals and some volumes of Shakespeare plays and sonnets. The bookends were religious figurines and beside one of these rested a pair of wire framed eye-glasses.

Steele closed the vestry door behind him and went to the table – emptied the water from the pitcher into the basin and stripped to the waist. There was no soap but the plain water felt good on his flesh, and he was able to clean off all but the most deeply ingrained dirt by vigorous scrubbing with a piece of fabric ripped from the largest cassock. He dried himself with the same cassock, put his shirt back on and then struggled into the smaller clerical garment: which was tight across the shoulders but otherwise fitted him well enough. The back to front collar was a perfect fit.

A grimacing glance into the mirror showed that he looked a very unlikely priest with his gaunt, thickly-stubbled face above the stark whiteness of the curved collar. But the two preachers who performed services at this church apparently shaved before they came early to smoke a pipeful of tobacco or read Shakespeare. The spectacles went some way to improving his appearance and were not too uncomfortable to wear – with plain glass in the right lens and producing a magnifying effect with the left. He gave another grin of satisfaction as he decided that he could have done worse after finding most of the town of Corinth in flames: and the Confederate army falling back from the Union advance.

At first, as he walked along the railroad tracks toward town, his intention had been to report to an appropriate member officer of General Beauregard's staff and thus make himself available for reassignment to duty. But then he had changed his mind. He was temporarily a free agent, able to do as he pleased within the limits imposed by a war situation in which not every man wore a Uniform to proclaim if he was friend or enemy. And as a free agent Lieutenant Adam Steele wanted no part of an army that was on the run – and from what he had seen and heard of recent events in the western theatre of operations, the Confederacy looked like being driven all the way back to the Gulf coast. So he had decided to strike out to the north or the east in search of some part of the Rebel army that was fighting and winning. But to have any hope of doing this he had to disguise his military identity, and he had crossed the final few yards into Corinth with no clear idea of how he would achieve this. Until sight of the church implanted this very idea and the contents of the vestry brought it to fruition.

A lone civilian wandering in the no-man's-land between opposing armies or coming within sight of pickets guarding a rest camp might arouse suspicion. But who would suspect a preacher?

Abruptly, gunfire crackled and in the mirror the Virginian saw his lips close and compress in front of his teeth. Then for long moments he remained where he was, at the table with his gloved hands hooked over the chairback. Listening to further shots, as they exploded closer than the initial fusillade. And guessed that a Union patrol had come within sight of Corinth, seen some of the Rebel rearguard and opened fire. Now fire was being returned and Steele knew he had to get out of the church and clear of the town fast. Before a greater number of Union troops closed in, maybe with artillery, to launch a full-scale attack on the unknown number of Confederates who remained amid the raging flames and billowing smoke that ravaged and polluted Corinth.

From the vestry window he was able to get a restricted view of the town side of the church and glimpsed two uniformed figures as they sprinted along a street: one a sharpshooter giving covering fire to the other, who hurled away a torch as he ran.

More shots were exploded from north of town, closer than before, and Steele moved away from the window and hurriedly pulled on the too large frock coat. He paused to

9

raise the hem of the cassock, drew the Colt from his army issue holster and transferred it to a pocket of the coat. The Derringer was in the other pocket.

About to leave the vestry, he hesitated again, then nodded and went to the bookshelf where he claimed one of the big Bibles. And now he did step out through the door and close it behind him: as the shooting from the north became louder and more incessant, while that from the south got sparodic and distant.

The closest north-facing window was by the pump organ and he went to this, dragging the stool against the wall so that he could climb on to it for a better view. His face expressed nothing of what he felt as he surveyed a straggling line of Union soldiers making for the cover of the church. Perhaps a score of them. With many more over to the east advancing on the area of the railroad depot and the section of town beyond. All of them carbine-toting infantrymen, methodically following the orders yelled by sabre-brandishing officers. By turns running, crouching, firing, reloading and lunging forward again. Exploding bullets wildly through the smoke and flames at unseen targets.

Some of the bullets thudded into the frame wall of the church and one of them shattered a window near the door. Whether any found the vulnerable flesh of retreating Confederate soldiers Steele had no way of knowing, for the sound of burning and shooting was clamorous enough to mask screams or yells.

But he did see three of the Yankees hit and fall, and just for a moment or two forgot about his predicament, to relish a surge of pleasure at witnessing these strikes against the enemy. And then came a sense of disappointment when one of the fallen rose up again and continued the advance.

Another window was smashed by a stray bullet and glass sprayed over the pews beneath. It was the window next to the one which was Steele's vantage point. He hurriedly climbed down from the stool and set it back by the organ.

'Fire . . . forward . . . down . . . reload . . . fire . . . forward and wipe the bastards off the face of the friggin' earth . . .'

Some of the Yankees had got close enough to the church for the Virginian to hear clearly the voice of an officer yelling commands. And, aware that he could use any kind of help – even divine – Steele bit back on a curse as he moved into the darkness beyond the arch behind the altar: with his left hand clutching the Bible and his right fisted around the cocked Colt in the pocket of the frock coat.

No more bullets thudded into the frame north wall of the church. But shoulders did. One, two, three, four – he gave up counting how many Yankees achieved the cover of the building.

'All right, boys! We done fine! The Captain's back there with a lousy hole in his head so I'm top man now!'

'It's a friggin' ill wind,' a voice responded sourly.

'Watch your lousy mouth, Turner!' came the retort. 'And all of you shift your stinkin' asses away from here! We come here to slaughter lousy Rebs, not praise the Lord! Reload and head out shootin'!'

'Sarge, I can't. I've got a bullet in the belly.'

'Hold on here, kid,' the sergeant growled and there was a note of pity in his voice. 'We'll come see to you soon as we done what we have to. Or maybe the whole company'll be here before that.'

'Sure, Sarge. Thanks.'

'Rest of you boys, go!'

Gunfire had continued to sound in the near and far distance while the men beside the church paused. Now it cracked immediately outside the walls, as some of the men ran around the front and some around the rear of the building.

'Down . . . reload . . . fire . . . forward . . .'

The non-com's orders rang out again. And faded along

131

with the sound of footfalls and shooting, as he and his platoon lunged deeper into the flaming town. Steele drew back his lips just fractionally in a cold grin of pleasure as he started to go around the altar: halted and drew back into the shadows as he heard an alien sound. A dragging sound, interspersed with thumps and gasps. Which after a few moments he identified as being caused by the wounded Yankee soldier, who was making slow and painful progress along the base of the north wall – heading for the front of the church.

Steele had not forgotten about the soldier whom the sergeant had called 'kid': but had considered him simply as an initial and minor obstacle in his path away from Corinth. He was still nothing more than that, as he unwittingly brought forward the time at which he had to be dealt with. Not evaded, as he might have been outside if it had been possible. For he was already struggling into the porch at the doorway which offered the only man-size entrance and exit in the church. Grunting and sucking in deep breaths as he forced himself to his feet.

The Virginian pursed his lips and stepped out of the shadows, around the altar and into the aisle. Held the Bible to his chest and tightened his grip around the butt of the Colt as he moved between the pews. Then came to a halt and had to make a conscious effort to spread a look of surprise and then compassion across his face, when the double doors crashed open and the wounded soldier lurched on to the threshold and gave a cry of alarm.

He was no more than eighteen. A tall, thin, clean-shaven youngster with black hair, deep-set eyes under a high forehead and a broad mouth above a sharp jaw. In the uniform of an enlisted man, at least two sizes too large for him. Using a carbine as a crutch when he entered, but quickly bringing it up to aim at Steele from the hip. This in a reflex action at seeing a possible enemy. An attitude he could not maintain because of the intense pain which seared through him from somewhere deep in his belly: behind the massive bloodstain that was still spreading across his tunic and pants. For a long second he expressed agony without voicing it. Then, as the carbine clattered to the floor and he sagged against the doorframe, the look changed to one of great shame. And he croaked:

'Oh, dear God, forgive me. Please, sir . . . I wouldn't've shot you . . . I didn't realise you were . . .'

'You're hurt,' Steele cut in as he started forward again.

'Bad, sir.' The young soldier tried to remain erect against the doorframe, but his legs buckled and he went down hard with a shrill scream. His legs were splayed and his head sagged down on to his chest: and when the scream ended Steele thought he had fainted. But then the pain-contorted young face was raised to show an expression of pleading to the fake preacher. 'So bad I'm gonna die, sir. You ain't a Catholic priest, are you?'

Steele halted a few feet from the Union soldier and shot a glance out through the doorway. He only saw flames, smoke and the blackened frameworks of partially destroyed buildings. No human figure moved among the ruins. The gunfire was all distant now.

'No. No, I'm not.' It was too terse, but when he looked down at the boy he saw no sign of distrust in the wide eyes.

'But can't you hear my confession, sir? We're all Christians, ain't we? Hear my confession and give me whatever kinda last rites you give?'

Perhaps there was time to offer some kind of solace to the mortally wounded youngster. It would not be valid, of course: but this boy would be unaware of the sacrilegious charade that was taking place – would die content about one aspect of his passing.

But what if he took too long to die? Remained alive for long enough to become aware of the trickery?

133

Steele scowled. That did not matter. The time element was important only to himself.

'Please, sir?' the boy pleaded, screwing his eyes tight shut as another wave of pain surged through him.

And the Virginian took a step closer and dropped to his haunches between the splayed legs of the soldier. And kept in the back of his mind the fact that this was a soldier. Age immaterial. A soldier in the Union army. While in the forefront of his mind he conjured up vivid images of the shattered corpses he had recently seen, sprawled across the gun-deck of the *Pride of Memphis* after the battle with the two Yankee ironclads.

'Hold this,' he said softly.

And the soldier opened his eyes and looked down at the Bible thrust toward him: gave a sigh of relief as he clutched the book in both his bloodstained hands. Then began to express depthless terror as he saw the gloved hands of the Virginian move and sensed menace. His grip on the Bible loosened and the book dropped to the floor. His mouth gaped wide to scream a denial of what was happening to him.

But the sound was trapped in his throat: as Steele's clutching hands found and tightened around his neck.

'If it helps, feller, I'm not a preacher,' the Virginian said huskily, gazing coldly into the terrified eyes of his victim. 'Lieutenant of the CSA cavalry.'

The hands of the helpless Yankee hooked over his wrists and fastened there tightly for long moments. Then weakened and fell away – as his tongue protruded from his lips, his complexion darkened and his eyelids widened to display great circles of white around the dark irises.

And suddenly it was done, the soldier a limp corpse which spasmed once as the last breath rattled from his throat when Steele eased his stranglehold.

For a moment the Virginian was gripped by a sense of

shame: as his eyes shifted from the bloated face to the blood-stain that evidenced the stomach wound. But then the distant sparodic gunfire suddenly intensified to a crackling fusillade and he snarled a curse and cleared his mind of irrelevant side issues.

And he went to work quickly – closing the dead soldier's eyes and mouth, pulling up his collar to conceal the neck bruises and then tipping him over on to his side. So that at first examination he would appear to have died of his wound – and perhaps at this time of many burials would be put into his grave without the true cause of his death ever being realised. Then he robbed the corpse. From the belt took the knife from the sheath and shells out of the ammunition pouch. And from the haversack on the dead man's back took a tin shaving cup with a cake of soap in it, a razor strop and a razor: left the flap unfastened so that it might appear that the equipment had been lost during the advance on Corinth.

Then, with the stolen knife strapped to his legs in the garter sheath and the rest of the loot distributed between the pockets of the frock coat, Steele retrieved the Bible and stood up.

And wrenching his gaze away from the face of the boy he had just murdered – found it drawn toward the altar at the end of the aisle. Felt shame threaten to well up inside him again and fought it with a snarl as he whirled around and then rasped: 'What the hell was I supposed to do? In here it all seemed heaven-sent!'

CHAPTER EIGHT

IT seemed like a long five months until mid-September and through that summer of 1862 Lieutenant Adam Steele covered a lot of miles: crossing Tennessee into North Carolina, and then heading up through his native Virginia toward the Potomac River.

His disguise served him well in evading capture by the Union forces pushing southward through western Tennessee, but he exchanged it at the first opportunity for an outfit of workaday clothes he found in an abandoned and partially burned homestead east of Chattanooga. And thus attired, was able to hire on as a casual hand from time to time as he made his slow way up the line of the Blue Ridge Mountains. He continued to wear the eyeglasses taken from the vestry of the church in Corinth and pretended to be acutely short-sighted – which allayed the suspicions of the more cautious farmers about such a young and able-bodied man not being in uniform.

The Potomac had not been the Virginian's destination at the outset of his long journey. And he changed his mind and direction several times between ploughing and planting and harvesting jobs on widely scattered isolated farmsteads: making his decisions on the strength of newspaper reports, or local gossip that seemed to have more than a grain of truth in it.

In the west he was leaving, the South suffered setback after setback. He heard about the abandonment of Fort Pillow and read about the Union blasting a way into Memphis – which augered badly for the states of Mississippi and Louisiana. While in the east, the war was going a good deal better for the Confederacy.

Stonewall Jackson hit the Yankees hard at Fort Royal and at Winchester in Virginia. Then routed the enemy at the battle of Cross Keys. After a seven day engagement, the northerners went into retreat from Oak Grove, Mechanics-ville, Gaines Mill, Savage Station, White Oak Swamp and Malvern Hill in Virginia – which forced the Yankees to abandon their advance on Richmond. Then the second battle of Manassas, or Bull Run as some newspapers called it, ended in a rout for the Union.

Steele read and listened avidly whenever the progress of the war was mentioned. And followed particularily closely the exploits of General Jackson and his command. For Stonewall was the man he was determined to serve under: and having decided upon this, he was able to justify to himself his absence from the western battlefronts where his orders said he should be.

Certainly he never considered himself a deserter as he pushed toward his objective, taking as much trouble to steer clear of CSA troops as he did to avoid patrols and concentrations of Union soldiers. And he maintained a kind of training programme designed to make him a better fighting soldier when the time to do battle came.

Mostly he practised with the knife, which he now carried in a leather sheath and harness he had fashioned for himself from some old horse tack he found in the barn of a place he worked on. He was able to practise his skill with this weapon at almost any time when he was not working, for it cost nothing and caused hardly any sound. So, with a carefully made and sewn slit in the outside seam of his right pants leg, he took every opportunity to crouch or raise his his leg so that the slit opened, draw the knife from the sheath and throw it at an inanimate target. It was a skill that appealed to him and he quickly discovered he had a natural talent for it.

He had far less aptitude for the Navy Colt, which came as no surprise to him. For although there had been hand-guns available back at the plantation, he had always pre-ferred to shoot with a rifle. But he persevered from time to time, when he had money to spare for bullets and the opportunity to fire the gun without arousing suspicion.

And on 17 September achieved his aim.

He had not worked for a week, during which he rode a newly purchased stallion to Harper's Ferry from Woodstock where he had earned the money in a livery stable. Harper's Ferry was his final destination, because of strong rumours that it was in this area that General Robert E. Lee planned to commence his invasion of the north, with the intention of going all the way to Washington. A prospect which was doubly alluring to the young lieutenant in civilian clothing because one of Lee's corps commanders was Stonewall Jackson.

He achieved his goal, but only just: racing his horse as fast as humanly possible over the final miles, with the sounds of battle crashing out ahead of him and muzzle flashes and billowing clouds of black powder smoke streaking and smudging the sky above the northern horizon.

Then the darkness of night clamped down over the Virginia-Maryland state line and a steady rain began to fall, reducing visibility and subduing sound. And in these con-ditions, galloping his stallion along a muddy turnpike to-wards the town of Sharpsburg, Steele almost ran down a staggering infantryman who flung a shrill-voiced obscenity

138

at the rider as he hurled himself into a ditch at the side of the road.

The Virginian brought his mount to a rearing, leg-flailing halt and leapt from the saddle: lost his footing in the mud and sprawled out on to his belly.

'What the frig you tryin' to do, you crazy sonofabitch?' the infantryman roared, as he crawled out of the ditch and struggled to his feet, clasping both hands to his right thigh where the fabric of his pants was stained with more than just mud.

Relieved that he had not killed the man, Steel rose up on to all fours and then came erect. Saw the man was a sergeant with broad shoulders, a short neck and a round face dominated by a bushy black moustache.

'Which army you with, Sergeant?' the Virginian snapped realising that the man's uniform tunic could be any colour under its coating of mud.

'What's it to you, civilian?' He accompanied the retort with a movement of his right hand. But even before his fingers reached the holster his face showed he had remembered it was empty.

By that time Steele had drawn the Navy Colt from a pocket of his frock coat and he took two steps toward the sergeant. Who looked afraid for a moment, then snarled defiantly:

'All right, Yank! One of your buddies started it! Finish me off if you gotta!'

The rain had washed off much of the mud from the man's tunic and Steele was close enough to see the grey colour of the fabric.

'Relax, Sergeant,' he said as he put away the revolver. 'We're on the same side. Robert E. Lee's having some trouble getting to Washington, uh?'

The man appeared indifferent to the fact that the threat of death had been removed. 'He ain't gotta chance, mister. The stinkin' bluebellies been givin' us a hidin' all day long.

From down out of East Woods and over Cemetery Hill. We never even got to smell the damn creek before the blue-bellies took the bridges and the fords. Crossed that stream and come at us like a solid wall. I was with Dan Hill's division. Got caught in the worst crossfire I ever did see. Out on the Sunken Road off the Boonsboro Turnpike. Hit us from the front and flank. I was lucky. Took this bullet in the leg but managed to crawl the hell out of there. Heard tell at the end of it that we lost so many killed you could walk that whole stretch of road and never put a foot on the ground. Bloody Lane is what they're callin' it now.'

'It's still going on, Sergeant,' Steele rasped, jerking a thumb over his shoulder in the direction from which the crash of artillery fire and the crackle of carbine and revolver shots was coming. 'Whatever happened to you and the rest of the men in your . . .'

'So go join in if you've a mind, mister,' the wounded non-com invited. 'Looked to me there's enough cannon fodder on both sides for this mess to go on for days. And a new recruit won't make much difference one way or the other. But count me out of this damn war for awhile. I've been holed up in Sharpsburg four hours waitin' to get my leg treated. But there just ain't enough medical officers or even ambulance men to go round all the wounded. So I'm fixin' to find me a doctor someplace to get this bullet out before the gangrene starts. Guess you ain't no doctor, mister?'

'Cavalry Lieutenant, Sergeant.'

The man expressed perplexity. Then asked: 'So what the hell you doin' chasin' around in . . ? Aw, hell, what does it matter to me? Unless you figure to shoot me down as a deserter. Which I ain't. But I'd rather take another bullet than go back to Sharpsburg. Rather be dead than face up to a field amputation. Leavin' now. Up to you what you do about it.'

He turned unsteadily and started off again along the turnpike in the rain, both hands still clutching his wounded thigh. And Steele watched him until he disappeared into the night, then turned himself and went to where the stallion waited: swung up into the saddle and heeled the animal forward into an easy walk.

There was dejection in his posture and the pace he set as he reflected on what the wounded non-com had reported: which made it appear that his long trip from the Mississippi to the Potomac had all been for nothing. He might just as well have rejoined Beauregard's command and fallen back before the Union advance, as come all the way here to share in what looked like being a defeat for the Confederacy, within striking distance of the major prize of Washington.

'Shouldn't go any further, mister,' a voice warned from Steele's right and he reined in his mount and peered into the trees on that side of the road.

'Who's there?' he asked.

'No one you'd know, but someone you'd better take heed of if you don't want to kill yourself.'

He stepped out on to the side of the road as he spoke, showing himself to be a grey uniformed infantry lieutenant. A match for Steele's height and build, but at least ten years his senior. With a weakly handsome face from which his eyes looked out as if nothing would ever surprise them. His clothing was sodden, he had lost his cap, and dried blood encrusted his hands which were gripping a .52 calibre Tarpley rifle.

'The shooting's died down a little,' he went on. Until this was pointed out, Steele had not realised that the sounds of the battle had subsided. There was no artillery fire now and just an occasional fusillade of small arms being exploded. 'But the whole thing could blow up again at any moment. Been like that most of the day.'

'Ain't it time we had some grub, sir?' a youthful voice called from deeper in the trees.

'Keep your eyes and your mind on your job, Land!' the lieutenant snapped over his shoulder.

'Then frig it, I'm gonna have a smoke! Maybe that'll help to keep my belly from . . . '

'No lights!' the lieutenant snarled, and whirled around.

A match flared and in its flame Steele saw the face of a young soldier with a cigarette jutting from the centre of his compressed lips. And an instant later the white of the cigarette paper was stained red by the torrent of blood that gushed from the gory wound where the man's nose had been.

The sound of the fatal gunshot cracked through the trees and the match fell, its fire extinguished by rain before it hit the sopping grass.

Other bullets exploded out of the darkness and other men screamed. In pain and anger and fear.

The lieutenant roared, 'Give it to them back, boys!'

And managed to cock and swing his rifle before two bullets tunnelled into his chest, sending him sprawling on to his back beside where Steele had started to lunge from his saddle.

Three gunshots exploded close by.

'You missed us, Johnnie Rebs!' a man roared triumphantly.

'Ain't you guys ever gonna admit you been beat?' This voice came from a different direction than the first.

'Only thing a redneck Southerner can ever whip is a bare assed nigger slave!' Yet another boastful Union man in another position. His taunt drawing gusts of laughter from at least six throats.

'Hold your fire!' Steele rasped, as he squatted beside the lieutenant and saw from the glazed stare in the man's eyes that he was dead.

If his words had registered, they were ignored. Three more shots were fired by the survivors of the lieutenant's troop. The Union sharpshooters drew a bead on the areas of the

142

muzzle flashes and triggered bullets toward known targets. Two of the Confederates were hit and the third shrieked an obscenity: and thus it was sound rather than light that brought rifle muzzles to bear on him – and his curse was ended by three rifles firing as one.

Steele had flung himself out full-length pressing himself against the soaking grass at the side of the road, right hand fisted around the frame of the lieutenant's Tarpley. Now he held his breath and listened intently. In the distance there was a burst of gunfire signifying another skirmish between pickets of the opposing armies. Close by, the Virginian could only hear the hiss and patter of falling rain. Then the sounds of men moving – going away from where he lay. Making small squelching noises and occasionally snapping a twig under a booted foot. And as he listened to the soldiers stealing away in search of fresh quarry, Steele's sense of relief at surviving was smothered by mounting anger.

The war was over a year old and it seemed that too many people had failed to learn anything about fighting it. Enlisted men still ignored their orders in such a highly dangerous situation as this and did insanely stupid things that got themselves and their comrades killed. While the group of Union marksmen who had taken such lethal advantage of the Confederate mistake had moved off without checking that all the enemy patrol were dead.

For a few seconds, as he lay in the mud with rain pelting his back, Adam Steele came close to throwing in his hand: as anger was displaced by depression, came back again and then seemed to be crushed by a burden of hopelessness too weighty to be lifted.

The rain continued to fall out of the dark sky, and for what seemed like a very long time only the sound of the man's and the horse's breathing counterpointed its constant hissing.

There were two armies stalled in the mud within hailing

distance of where he lay. One defending the approach to the seat of its government; the other set upon reaching this vitally important objective.

So what the hell were the crazy bastards in command doing? Were they scared of the dark? Or reluctant to get their heads wet?

A single shot cracked out. And a man screamed. Perhaps a half mile away.

These two sounds spurred Steele to precise and un-hurried action.

First, robbery of the dead again: as he stripped the body of the lieutenant of his uniform and equipment. And donned the clothing after shedding his own, feeling nothing as his gloved fingers carefully fastened the buttons of the bullet-holed and bloodstained tunic.

Then he buckled the dead man's belt around his waist, checked the Dance Brothers .44 revolver in the holster and slid the sabre from the scabbard to test its feel. Next he used its honed point to slit the seam in the uniform pants. And completed his preparations by fashioning a rifle boot from his old pants and tying this to the saddlehorn, Tarpley inside, before swinging up astride the stallion. Finally Steele stroked the horse's neck and drawled, 'All right, feller. Let's go show old Robert E. Lee how to fight a fucking war.'

And as he heeled his mount into movement and tugged on the reins to steer him off the turnpike and into the trees, it did not cross his mind that he was acting like a selfish and spoilt child again.

Which proved to be the salvation of a certain Sergeant Curtis Oatman.

'Let's cut his ears off first, you guys.'

'No, turn him over and slice his ass like it was a Thanks-giving turkey.'

'Finish me off quick, you sonsofbitches!'

The voices came out of the hissing rain as disembodied

sounds, two in a tone of evil glee and the third shrill with anger. Ahead and to the right of where Steele brought his horse to a halt, some ten minutes after leaving the turnpike.

'That's it, Reb! Beg for mercy! But do it right! Up on your friggin' knees!'

This from another Union man, taunting the helpless Confederate who spoke with the same Virginian drawl as Steele.

'You ain't gonna get none, Sergeant.' This rasped by a fourth tormentor. 'I say we start by hackin' off his balls.'

'So quit talkin' about it and do it!' the lone Confederate snarled.

'Nice to have the invite.'

Steele drew the revolver, thumbed back the hammer and thudded his heels into the flanks of the stallion. The threatened soldier vented a stream of shrill obscenities. But no human voice could have shouted loud enough to mask the thud of the stallion's hooves as Steele galloped his mount clear of the trees.

Five faces were turned toward him, as he showed himself on a swathe of mire-like grassland between the timber and a rushing stream. One of the men sprawled out on the ground with his head and shoulders propped against a boulder, his hands interlocked over the centre of a great bloodstain that covered the area of his belly and upper thighs. In front of the gut-shot Confederate sergeant was a line of four Union men with knives clenched in their fists.

Other faces were also turned toward the newcomer and some were not. But they did not matter since they wore the frozen expressions of men who were long dead. Confederates all – perhaps a dozen of them. Some with broken bodies from shell fire, and others marked only by the wounds of the bullets which had ended their lives.

The Virginian only caught a fleeting impression of this scene of carnage surrounding the three craters exploded by artillery shells. Then he added fresh horror as he pulled up his galloping mount and, while the animal reared, exploded two bullets from the revolver.

One Yankee went down with both hands clutching at his face, as if the man were trying to stem the gush of blood that erupted from a wound below his right eye. Then another was hit in the heart and did a complete turn before collapsing on to the ground.

'Jesus Christ!' somebody screamed.

'Atta boy!' the wounded sergeant yelled.

The Union man who had blasphemed hurled away his knife, whirled and raced toward the stream. While the fourth Yankee dropped to his haunches, transferred his knife from the right to the left hand and drew his revolver.

But was momentarily blinded by a spray of mud that splashed into his face from the forehooves of the stallion as it crashed back to the ground. And Steele elected to slide his own revolver back into the holster and put a newly learned skill to the test – delved a hand through the gaping split in his pants leg, drew the knife and turned his mount before setting the blade spinning toward a target.

'Damnit, I did it!' he roared in elation when he saw the knife sink to the hilt in the chest of the soldier.

'Get the last one, Lieutenant!' the sergeant shrieked. 'Don't let the bastard . . .'

Gunfire sounded and a hail of bullets cracked out of the rainy night to smack into tree trunks, splinter rock from boulders and tunnel into muddy turf. And with a scream the wounded Confederate went over into a roll. Whether the sound was of pain or fear or whether he was seeking to become less of a target, Steele did not know.

For he had turned the stallion again and demanded another gallop. Less concerned with the bullets cracking through the air around him than the last of the quartet of Union soldiers who was staggering across the white stream.

He felt invincible. For months he had trekked across the war-ravaged eastern states to seek a battle that would end in a decisive victory for the Confederacy, and had found only another stalemate. So he had declared his own private war, and against the odds had finished three fourths of the enemy's strength.

Now, despite covering fire, he was on the track of the last fourth. And was determined to bring down this man, too. With the ease of an experienced huntsman, ahead of the pack, claiming the honour of killing the quarry.

But there were no dogs and although he had access to a rifle, he elected not to make use of it. Instead, he drew the sabre. And brandished it about him like some warrior of a bygone age.

The man was shouting something as the horse carried Steele level with him. While the wounded sergeant proclaimed that he was still alive by shrieking at the top of his voice. But no words reached the Virginian's ears clearly. He heard only his own rapid breathing and the splashing of hooves in the stream.

Then he leaned to the side and aimed the sabre at his target, as the final motion of the brandishing sequence. And was unaware of the involuntary whoop of delight that burst from his throat as he felt the momentary resistance to the blade: saw the head decapitated from the neck, a fountain of warm blood splattering his head and wrist and forearm.

The horse galloped on and the rider did not look back. Held the sabre low, so that the spray splashing from under the pumping hooves washed blood from the blade.

Bullets snagged at his clothing and he threw back his head and responded with a gust of laughter as he thrust the sabre back into the scabbard. Only to be jerked back to his senses when one shot from out of the rain-lanced darkness took the heel off his right boot.

And only then did he wrench over the reins to angle the

racing stallion away to the left: out of the stream and across churned-up turf. Felt the more solid ground of a road under the thundering hooves. Stayed on the road with the gunfire at his back. Experienced the familiar sensation of fear as he leaned forward in the saddle, side of his head pressed to the neck of the horse.

Then heard gunfire from another direction. Looked up and saw muzzle flashes directly ahead. But realised just before he was about to veer his mount off the road that the riflemen ahead were not aiming at him. Rather, they were providing covering fire – seeking to silence the guns of the Union soldiers until he raced out of no-man's-land and reached the comparative safety of the area behind the Confederate lines.

Where he would learn that he had added four to a casualty list which, when tallied, would prove to be a bloody record. For the road he was on was called the Boonsboro Turnpike and the fast-running stream in which he had beheaded a Union soldier was Antietam Creek: giving its name to a battle in which both sides lost more men in a single day than any other in the war.

But it was not until many years later that his reckless rescue of Sergeant Curtis Oatman from the sadistic Yankees was to register as more than one violent incident among many. When, in the Snake Mountains of distant Nevada Territory, Oatman would be in a position to return the favour.*

For the present, as he galloped through the Confederate picket line and slowed his horse with the exchange of shots losing its frantic intensity, only one train of thought occupied the Virginian's mind.

He had done some killing and had done it well. But in indulging his lust for this brand of self-gratification he could have had little if any effect on the outcome of this

* *Adam Steele 10 — The Losers*

battle, the conduct of which had spurred him to action. And
he had rejoined the army from which he had taken an un-
authorised leave of absence. Rejoined it far from that part
of the country where his orders said he should be: a cavalry
lieutenant attired in the uniform of a dead infantry officer.

He walked his horse between buildings and saw that he
was in a small town – a sign above a storefront showing it
was Sharpsburg.

A door across the street was flung open and a wedge of
light stabbed out into the rainy night.

'Mister!' a man roared harshly. 'Just what the hell do you
think you've been at?'

Steele reined in his mount and squinted at the silhouetted
figure in the lighted doorway, saw the insignia of a major
on the man's tunic and raised a hand in a weary salute.

'Lieutenant Adam Steele reporting for duty, sir,' he said,
and swung down from the saddle.

'We'll get to your name later, mister!' the major snapped.
'I asked you what the hell you've been playing at!'

The Virginian kept his voice low as he angled across the
street towards the incensed senior officer and rasped, 'I
guess you could say I've been playing many parts, feller.'

THE PREACHER

Part Two

'DEARLY beloved, we are gathered here in the sight of God, and in the face of this congregation to . . .'

The Reverend Saul M. Jarvis looked up from the prayer book held in his two hands and gazed beyond Adam Steele and Lucy Girard casting his small, sunken eyes over the unseeing and unhearing congregation. And made a choking sound deep in his throat as he broke off from reading.

'Easy, feller,' the Virginian said, as the woman at his side squeezed his right arm with tense fingers. 'Keep your mind on what you're doing.'

Jarvis stared at Steele and the woman, thoughts elsewhere for a second or so, then nodded and cleared his throat. 'Yes. Yes, sir. I'm sorry.' He returned his nervous gaze to the open prayer book and continued, ' . . . congregation, to join together this man and this woman in Holy . . .'

His voice got stronger and after a few moments his hands ceased to tremble. And Steele felt confident that the preacher would be able to get through the marriage ceremony without going to pieces.

It was mid-afternoon now and he, Lucy and Jarvis were alone on the San Simon Rancheria: enacting the wedding service before the sprawled bodies of the slaughtered cavalry-men. They stood at the rear of the preacher's shack, the heat of the glaring sun alleviated a little by a slight breeze that moved their hair, eddied dust about their feet and wafted the stench of dead and rotting flesh under their nostrils.

The shack and the Indian Agency building were the only substantial signs which remained of the Apache rancheria, for the Mescaleros had dismantled and hauled away the wickiups when they left. The communal cooking fire had long since gone out, and its ashes had been picked up and scattered across the dusty ground on which the dead were decomposing.

They had made haste to leave, but with the elderly and frail Chief Red Bull in authority again after the slaughter of the Fort Blading soldiers, there had been no panic. And those braves – among them the chief's twin sons – who were in favour of leaving Jarvis and the two white eyes strangers as dead as the cavalrymen, were overruled.

They were confined to the preacher's house, under guard, while the Apaches made preparations to leave: and it was during this period of imprisonment and inactivity that Adam Steele found himself reflecting on the events which had filled so much of his time during the war year of 1862. Memories doubtless triggered by the slaughter of the troopers and the presence in the cramped shack of this unlikely looking preacher.

While he sat on the floor, knees folded up to his chest, back against the wall and hat tipped forward over his face, Lucy slept fitfully on the narrow bed and Jarvis began to take guilty sips from a whiskey bottle. Then, by the time the Indians were ready to leave, the woman was in a deep and exhausted sleep, the preacher was sprawled face down across the table muttering intermittently in a drunken stupor induced by two bottles of liquor and the Virginian was wallowing in a morass of remorse: his mind crowded with memories of dead women and children, the mortally wounded soldier he had strangled, the recklessly brave Major Garner, Gloria the Attrill whore who had died to save him, the old blind ferryman and his granddaughter who . . .

'We go now, white eyes,' another old man said, breaking in on Steele's melancholic train of thought. And the Virginian tilted the hat back on his head to squint at Red Bull standing on the threshold of the sunlit doorway. 'We leave you to tell other pony-soldiers from the fort what has happened here. And I ask that you tell something else. I, Red Bull, have spoken with the brave known as Joe Starlight. And he has sworn to our Gods that he did not do that which has been said he done. I accept his word on this.'

Steele rose to his feet and nodded. 'I'll see the message is delivered. But it won't make any difference after what happened today.'

Now the old chief nodded. 'This I know, white eyes. I did not know that the braves had gathered weapons and were holding secret war councils. Readying themselves to do battle with the pony-soldiers when I am dead.'

Disillusion showed in every line of his wrinkled face until the Virginian offered: 'I'll tell them that, too.'

Red Bull became grimly resolute. 'That does not matter, white eyes. What is done is done. And while I live I will be as one with my people. Too old to ride a war pony and carry arms. But I will do what I can. Just tell that it was a false accusation which aroused the anger of my people. And that we will spill the blood of many more white eyes along the trail we ride. For after today we know that the only peace we will ever find is in our graves.'

He turned from the doorway and disappeared from sight. And Steele approached the threshold of the shack, looked first at his gelding which was tethered on the shady side of the building – saw that the highly prized Colt Hartford rifle with the inscribed gold plate screwed to the fire-scorched stock jutted from the forward slung boot. Then, with lips pursed, he watched as the old chief was assisted astride a pony by his sons. Who mounted their own animals and allowed their father to take the head of the column. Which moved off at a hand signal, trailing dust raised by the unshod hooves of Apache ponies and the shod ones of the confiscated cavalry horses.

He watched the string of riders until they were blurred by heat shimmer down in the valley, and then faded out of sight. He went back inside the shack and allowed Lucy Girard to sleep her sleep. Asked, as soon as she awoke:

'Do you still want to get married?'

'They've gone?'

'Just us and the dead left.'

'I want to get away from here.'

'Married people can still be single-minded, Lucy.'

She swung her feet to the floor and pointed to Jarvis. 'The preacher, he looks . . .'

'He's dead drunk is all. Reckon we all have our own ways of living with ourselves. You get yourself ready and I'll light a fire, fix some coffee.'

He did this, while the woman did the best she could in the circumstances to freshen herself up after sleep. Then Steele roused Jarvis and forced hot, strong coffee into him. And the more sober the preacher became, the greater became his fear – of the Apaches having a change of heart and coming back to kill them, and of a search party of soldiers riding out from Blanding and accusing him of complicity with the Indians in the slaughter of their comrades. He was certainly in no mood to conduct a marriage ceremony, until the Virginian reminded him his liquor supply was exhausted and he would not have the opportunity or the money to re-plenish it unless he did what was asked of him.

So now the trio stood in the freshening breeze behind the shack, the smell of death in their nostrils and the preacher's words sounding clearly in their ears. And first Adam Steele and then Lucy Girard answered 'I will' in response to Jarvis's enquiries read from the prayer book.

'Who giveth this woman . . . ' he made to continue, and broke off to look up, afraid again. 'We don't have anyone to give the bride to you, sir. Or a best man. Or a ring. We can't proceed.'

Steele sighed softly. 'No banns were published and there was no one around to allege impediment, feller. Do the best you can.'

'I have a ring,' Lucy offered, and delved a hand into the front of her dress to produce a gold band. 'It was my mother's. I swore to her that when I got married I would use . . . '

'Dear God in heaven, the soldiers are coming,' Jarvis rasped.

Both Steele and the woman looked over their shoulders and saw a body of uniformed men, riding fast along the trail which the first ill-fated patrol had followed earlier in the day.

'Finish it, feller,' Steele snapped as he returned his attention to the preacher, and picked the ring off Lucy's sweat tacky palm.

'I don't . . . ' Jarvis's hands and voice were both trembling.

'Just do it!' the Virginian ordered, as the woman stared at the preacher, confused by the extent of his nervousness.

Jarvis swallowed hard and cleared his throat. Blurted: 'Repeat after me. I Adam take thee Lucy to my wedded wife . . . '

The sound of hoofbeats could be heard now and the preacher spoke faster. While first Steele and then Lucy responded in measured tones.

'Clasp hands!'

They did so.

And Jarvis laid his right hand upon theirs and said quickly: 'Those whom God hath joined together let no man

155

put asunder. I now pronounce you man and wife. You may kiss the bride.'

Steele did so, brushing his lips lightly across the warm and moist cheek of his wife, as the cavalrymen reined in their galloping mounts and a man bellowed, 'What in frigging hell is happening here?'

'A wedding, captain,' the Virginian answered, as he and Lucy turned to look across the humped forms of the dead soldiers to the score or so living ones.

'Don't you frigging smart-talk me, mister!' the middle-aged captain snarled, livid with shock and anger. 'Preacher-man, how come these men are dead? Where are the red-skins?'

Jarvis snapped the prayer book closed and held it in both hands, pressed to his heaving chest, as he blurted out an account of the slaughter. This as a half dozen troopers swung down from their saddles and carried out grim-faced checks of the dead.

'And these two strangers?' the captain asked when the preacher was through. 'What kind of people are you – getting married in such surroundings as these?'

He swung his gaze from the sweating face of Jarvis to the impassive features of the Virginian.

'He forced me to . . . ' the preacher began.

'Planned to have this feller marry us before your boys showed up, captain,' Steele cut in. 'Nothing we could do to help them once they were dead. So reckoned to go through with . . . '

'They headed west into the valley, sir,' a hawk-faced corporal reported after going around to the front of the shack and spotting signs of the Apaches' trail.

The captain had been looking at Steele with blatant revulsion. Now he acknowledged the non-com's information with a curt nod and began to issue orders: commanding four men to track the Apaches, despatching one back to

156

Blanding to report what had happened, and sending others to wrap the dead in blankets and load them on to horses. Then he returned his attention to the Virginian and depthless contempt glowed dully in his eyes.

'Get out of my sight, mister!' he snarled. 'And take your woman with you. We'll get those murdering redskins, no help from you. And every last one of them will pay for what's happened here. May your married life be long and miserable for what you didn't do here.'

'It was what someone did do that led to this, captain,' Steele said. 'Go bring the horse, Lucy.'

She was glad to be gone, conscious that the ill-feeling expressed by the officer and many of the men was directed as much at her as at her new husband.

'Just what is that supposed to mean, mister?' the captain barked.

'Joe Starlight didn't rape and kill the wife of one of the Fort Blanding men is what it means.' And waited for the harsh sounds of the troopers' jeers to subside before adding: 'Red Bull told me to tell you that Joe Starlight denied it and he believes him.'

This time the response from the uniformed men was louder and harsher, and had to be silenced by a snarled order from the captain. Who sneered contemptuously into the abrupt silence, 'The Indian was seen close to the fort the night it happened, mister! By a patrol of men under the command of a lieutenant. White men, mister. Whose word I would accept against that of a thousand Apaches!'

Lucy came around the shack with the horse and gave the reins to Steele. Murmured, 'I left my bag inside, Adam.'

'Don't know enough about the killing to speak on that, captain,' the Virginian answered. 'But I reckon it's more often than not a fact that a drunken man speaks the truth.'

'Drunken man . . ?' the captain rasped. 'Truth? Truth about what?'

'Don't, Mr Jarvis!' Lucy screamed.

Steele whirled into a half-turn, as every trooper swung his gaze away from the Virginian to stare at the corner of the shack. Where the woman came into view, rigid with fear and walking backwards. Retreating from the Reverend Saul M. Jarvis. Who had gone into his crude home and exchanged the prayer book for a Colt Navy Model revolver of uncertain age. Which he carried low down, at arm's length on his right side.

'No, my dear,' he said dully. 'Don't be afraid of me. I don't intend to harm anybody.'

Steele stepped behind the woman who gasped when she bumped into him. Then became limp with relief and might have collapsed to the breeze-stirred dust had he not encircled her waist with an arm. Jarvis came to a halt and swept his watery-eyed gaze over the surprised faces of the troopers.

'A man gets lonely living out in a place like this,' he said and there was a pleading for understanding in his voice and his face. 'I am not of the Church of Rome and the pleasures of the flesh are not forbidden. Perhaps if my ministry among the heathen Apaches had been more successful that would have been enough. But I have failed. And I sought solace in liquor. It was not enough. It served only to sharpen my needs. That night when Mrs Helga Traynor approached me for spiritual guidance – I misjudged her and thought . . . Realised too late that she was not encouraging me. She threatened to disgrace me. I felt I had to silence her. It seemed the only way.'

He started to bring up the revolver and looked with deep sadness in his eyes at Steele and Lucy. 'My sleep was troubled, I suppose. My guilty conscience forced me to unwittingly confess my terrible crime.'

'Preacherman!' the captain roared.

'No,' Lucy gasped.

158

And shrieked in alarm as Steele pushed her forcefully away from him, and dropped fast on to his haunches – right hand delving in a blur of speed through the gaping slit in his pants leg. His movements faster than those of the troopers who clawed for the guns in their holsters.

'Forgive me, my God!' Jarvis shouted to the sky.

The knife was out of the sheath and Steele had drawn his arm back to start a swing that would spin the blade toward the man. But he checked the action. Saw Jarvis snap his head down so that his chin rested on his chest – as the gun in his hand rose and was twisted. The muzzle was thrust into the gaping mouth and the trigger was squeezed.

The report of the gunshot was muffled. But the gruesome effect could be seen in stark clarity: as the bullet, exploded from such short range, burst clear through the top of the man's head in a spray of crimson flecked with white bone fragments and he toppled backwards, hand falling away from the butt while the gun stayed in his mouth, its barrel held in the death-grip of the teeth.

The arid ground thirstily soaked up the spilled blood. And windblown dust adhered to the massive wound in the skull, dulling the crimson brightness.

'Goodness, Adam,' Lucy gasped.

'And evil,' the Virginian murmured, as he replaced the knife in the sheath and straightened up. 'Reckon there's some of each in all of us.'

He beckoned for her to mount the gelding, and because she was shaken by shock he had to help her.

'You men carry out your orders!' the captain snapped. 'This matter won't be closed until Red Bull and every one of his braves has paid the price of this slaughter!'

'Adam,' the new Mrs Steele said, as the troopers responded to the command and the Virginian started to lead the gelding away from the shack with the new corpse beside it. 'If Jarvis had confessed this morning, all this could have been avoided.'

'Delayed is all, I reckon,' he answered. 'The braves had guns and where just waiting for the old chief to die. Way things are between most Indians and most whites, the killing won't ever be over. There's just no . . .

... END TO IT.'*

* There is to this account of Adam Steele's past and present life, but it will be continued in the next book of the series.